Sea Change

Sea Change

LINDA SMITH

THISTLEDOWN PRESS

Canadian Cataloguing in Publication Data
Smith, Linda, 1953–
Sea change
ISBN 1-895449-86-3
I. Title.
PS8587.M5528 S4 1999   C813'.54   C99-920055
PZ7.S65425 Se 1999

Cover painting by Rand Walsh
Typeset by Thistledown Press
Printed and bound in Canada

Thistledown Press Ltd.
633 Main Street
Saskatoon, Saskatchewan
S7H 0J8

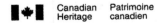

Thistledown Press gratefully acknowledges the financial assistance of the Canada Council for the Arts, the Saskatchewan Arts Board, and the Government of Canada through the Book Publishing Industry Development Program for its publishing program.

Sea Change

CONTENTS

ATUA

MORIA

The Circle

The story so far

Wind *Shifter*, the first book of *The Freyan Trilogy*, tells the story of fourteen year old Kerstin Speller's encounter with the Ugliks, the traditional enemies of her country, Freya. Kerstin is apprenticed to her father Morgan, a powerful wizard, and dreams of being the greatest wizard since Mika, the legendary hero of the Uglik War fought five centuries earlier. But her dreams are frustrated by the time it takes to look after the household, which she has done since her mother's death. It angers her that her fellow apprentice, Alaric Thatcher, does not help with the work and is surpassing her in his studies.

Then Morgan leaves with his friend Ben Grantwish on a voyage to the Misty Isles, whose inhabitants are said to have strong magical gifts, especially in healing. During his absence, a drought strikes the land . . . Messengers arrive from the king, summoning Morgan to a council in the capital city, Freybourg. Ugliks have been sighted in the high hills, and some teachers at the College of Wizards believe that Ugliks have caused the drought. Alaric and Kerstin persuade the messengers to take them to Freybourg in Morgan's absence. At the council, it is decided to send an army of warriors and wizards into the hills. Kerstin is furious when she discovers that, although Alaric is allowed to accompany this army, she is forbidden. Determined to use a spell of invisibility to spy on the enemy, she runs away from the palace and sets off into the hills by herself.

Kerstin does locate an enemy band, but realises, to her dismay, that she cannot discover their secrets because they speak a foreign language. Then her beloved pony, Sybilla, is captured. Trying to free her, Kerstin herself is caught. An attempted flight ends in her pony's death and her own recapture. She is taken through a tunnel to Uglessia, and there left at the home of Yrwith, a woman who has tried to use an old spell to change the pattern of the winds and so bring much-needed rain to Uglessia. Unfortunately, her spell has gone wrong, resulting in a drought for Freya and torrential rain for Uglessia.

Like most Freyans, Kerstin has been raised on tales of the Uglik War, and believes all Ugliks, or Uglessians, as they call themselves, are ugly, cruel and treacherous. Her beliefs are challenged by the poverty she sees around her and her hosts' kindness. She has inherited her mother's gift of "true dreams" that show her present and future events. Aided by a dream that allows her to know Alaric's real feelings, she comes to understand that the truth behind individuals' and countries' behaviour is more complex than she had thought, and that Freyans were as much to blame as Uglessians for the Uglik War.

She returns to Freya armed with a counter-spell that will restore rain to Freya, and determined to help Uglessia by permanently shifting the winds and giving the land more rain. She is received as the heroine she has dreamed of being. But when she broaches the idea of sending aid to Uglessia, only Alaric stands with her. In the end, help is given, but only after Kerstin threatens to withhold the spell that would end the drought. The book concludes with Kerstin and Alaric under strong official disapproval. But they understand each other better, and they know they have helped Uglessia.

ATUA

PLANS

The man on the bed moaned. His head moved restlessly; his eyes roved, dulled, unfocused, around the hut. Kerstin knelt and took his hand, holding it firmly, willing him to look at her, willing him to be still, to be well. His eyes strayed to her face, stayed, clung. She held his hand more closely, feeling the fever that raged through his body, feeling the hard earth beneath her knees. Beyond the hut's open door, rain fell in a gentle mist. A cool breeze blew in through the open window, rustling the curtains, touching the hair of the girl asleep in the high-poster bed. Kerstin stirred, murmured drowsily, then opened her eyes to early morning sunshine washing her room. She lay, blinking, as the dream faded. The hut, the man on the bed, herself, holding his hand, healing . . . only a dream.

Then she remembered.

Ben Grantwish should arrive today. He and her father would finalise their plans. Soon — soon — they would be on their way, sailing over the sea to the Misty Isles.

A dream, yes. But a dream based on reality. A dream that would soon come true.

Kerstin scrambled out of bed. Grabbing a dress, she pulled it over her head, then spared a quick glance at the small mirror that hung on her wall. A round face with a snub nose, level eyebrows and a stubborn chin met her gaze. Hastily, she dragged a comb through her flyaway brown hair, then went over to the window and leaned out.

From her room high in the old house on Wizard's Hill, she could see the path winding down the hill to the town of Frey-by-the-Sea sprawled at its foot. Beside the town, the River Frey, a massive, slow-moving giant, rolled to its home in the sea. And there, sparkling beyond the river and the town, was the sea itself, the sea they would be sailing over in just a few days. Well, maybe a week.

Eyes shining, she drew in her head, then left her room and bounded down the stairs that twisted and turned their way to the ground floor.

The tangy smell of *kala* met her as she entered the kitchen. She sniffed, wishing she liked the taste of *kala* as much as its smell. But perhaps she only liked the smell so much because it reminded her of Uglessia. Strange to think that if she had never gone to Uglessia, *kala* would be unknown in Freya. Now, only two years after her contact with the Uglessians, most Freyans were willing to pay a high price to drink the hot, rather bitter brew.

Alaric was standing in front of the wood stove, absently stirring a pot of oatmeal while reading the book he held in one hand. Kerstin grinned. Alaric was no more interested in cooking and housework than she was. But at least he did his fair share now, though not without an occasional grumble.

"How many lumps in that porridge?"

Alaric jumped. "I didn't hear you coming."

"Sorry. Is breakfast almost ready?"

He peered into the pot. "I think so. There are some lumps," he admitted.

Kerstin shrugged. "I've eaten lumpy porridge before." She got a bowl and helped herself.

Alaric joined her at the table with his own bowl and a cup of *kala*.

"How you can drink that! . . . "

"It's an adult taste. You'll enjoy it when you're older," he told her kindly.

Kerstin made a face at him. Ever since becoming her father's apprentice, Alaric had never let her forget that he was two and a half years older than she was.

"You're not that old, Alaric Thatcher."

"Nineteen," he said smugly. True. He had turned nineteen a couple of weeks ago, while Kerstin had seven months to go before she was seventeen. She scowled at him, then asked, "Is Father down yet?"

"No, Morgan's still sleeping. It's early yet," he added, seeing her surprise.

"I suppose it is. I'm too excited to sleep very late these days," she confessed.

"Hmmm." He took a sip of *kala*, then smiled a bit sheepishly. "Me too."

Kerstin smiled back. "It won't be long now."

"No."

They ate in silence for a few minutes. Then Alaric asked, "What do you think they'll be like? The Misty Isles, I mean. Oh, I've heard Morgan's and Ben's tales, but . . . Will they welcome us, do you think? The Wise Women?"

"They told Father and Master Grantwish they could return to learn more of their magic."

"Yes, but . . . Do you think they'll really clear a path through the mist for us?"

"Captain Merrigale must think they will, or he wouldn't risk sailing his boat through it."

"Captain Merrigale has already wrecked two ships landing on the Misty Isles," Alaric pointed out dryly. "I wouldn't call that a reassuring record."

"He didn't wreck them, only damaged them."

"Mmmm."

Hamish Merrigale's first landing on the Misty Isles had been accidental. Driven there by a freak storm, he had come home with tales of white-robed women who possessed strange, powerful magic — tales that led Morgan

Speller and Ben Grantwish to accompany him on his second expedition to the mysterious, fog-enshrouded islands. On both trips, Captain Merrigale's ships had been gouged by rocks invisible in the fog.

"The Wise Women taught Father and Master Grantwish to mind-call so that they could ask for safe passage."

"I know." Alaric stirred his porridge. Kerstin studied his bent head, his fine-boned, serious face. A strand of reddish-gold hair had fallen onto his forehead. His blue-green eyes were hidden by long lashes. She frowned.

"Then why — "

"I don't . . . Oh, it's not the fog that worries me, not really, though anyone with any sense would have to be at least a little fearful of it. It's . . . I know the Wise Women told Morgan and Ben they could return — though a bit grudgingly, from the sound of it. But they don't know we — you and I — are coming. I don't think they'll be glad to see me."

Kerstin stared at him. "Why not?"

"Because I'm a man. There are no men on the island, according to Ben and Morgan. The Wise Women will probably see me as just another male intruder, to be tolerated at best." He considered this, frowning, then added, "They may welcome you, though, since you're female like them."

"Good."

"Good for you, maybe."

Kerstin tossed her head. "It's high time things were reversed. How do you think I feel, having everything in Freya run by men?"

"That's not true."

"No? How many women do you know who are town councillors or army officers or wizards?"

"There are a few female wizards."

"How many?"

He thought for a minute. "Not many," he conceded.

"That's right. Women are expected to look after households and have babies, not concern themselves with town business, or affairs of state, or magic."

"I do my share of the housework," he protested.

"Now you do." There had been a time when this had not been true, and Kerstin had resented it terribly. "But, Alaric, don't you

21

want to go to the Misty Isles? I thought . . . You fought as hard as I did to persuade Father to let us go."

She watched him anxiously as he mashed an especially large lump of porridge against the side of his bowl. Surely he wanted to go, to share this experience, to learn, with her, the Wise Women's magic.

He raised his head, pushed the errant hair off his forehead, and gave her a swift smile. "Of course I do. I've wanted to see the islands ever since Captain Merrigale told us about his first voyage there, and especially since Morgan and Ben returned from their visit two years ago."

Kerstin's spirits rose again and bubbled over into an excited laugh. She gazed in front of her but she saw, not the rosewood table, not the young man sitting across from her, but a small round hut where a kneeling woman held the hand of a man tossing and burning with fever. Then the woman's magic worked, and the man stilled and settled into healing sleep, while, beyond the open door, rain fell like a misty curtain.

Two years ago, she had seen that hut and that woman in a true dream, the first true dream she had ever had. And this morning she had dreamed of that hut once more. Only this time, it had been she who had been kneeling by the sick man, she who had been the healer. It had not been a true dream this time. She knew that. It had not been vivid enough, concrete enough. But might it not forecast the future anyway?

Soon, they would land on those islands of mist and mystery. Until a few years back, she had thought them fairy tales, stories sailors told to amuse children. But they were real, those islands, and the magic on them was real, too — real and powerful, more powerful than anything known in Freya.

"Just think what the Wise Women can teach us, Alaric. Think what we can learn from them. Mind-speech. Healing. When I think about it — " She stopped and shook her head in wonder, then said solemnly, "I think the Wise Women will change our lives."

Message from Uglessia

Kerstin squirmed in her wooden chair, unable to concentrate on the book in front of her, even though it was *Spells of Wind and Weather*, which she usually found fascinating. She peered out the study window into the empty, tangled garden lit by the late afternoon sun. Where was Ben Grantwish? He should be here by now.

She looked over at her father. Morgan seemed tranquilly absorbed in the book he was reading. Alaric, though, was as fidgety as she was. They exchanged glances, then sighed in unison.

Morgan glanced up, a gleam of amusement in his dark eyes. "Impatient? He'll get here when he gets here. Even then, it will be at least a week before we can set sail."

"I know," Kerstin said gloomily. "All the same — " She broke off, hearing the thud of horses' hooves. A minute later, the bell that hung by their garden gate rang.

Despite his calm demeanour, Morgan was the first one on his feet and out the door. Kerstin and Alaric followed on his heels.

"Ben!" Morgan greeted his old friend joyously, then stopped, seeing the stranger beside him.

"Freyn's Day to you, Morgan. Please meet Master Vern Bourgly. He tells me he knows Kerstin and Alaric, and has a message for your daughter. We met on the boat coming down from Freyfall."

"Freyn's Day, Master Bourgly." Morgan extended a cordial hand and ushered the two men into the garden.

Kerstin smiled at the younger man and bobbed a quick curtsy, then turned to Ben Grantwish, who had been a friend since her childhood. She hesitated a moment, then decided to ignore adult decorum. She flung her arms around him. He returned the hug enthusiastically.

"We've been waiting forever for you."

"I got here as quickly as the boat and this sorry nag would bring me," he protested. "You rent slow horses in Frey-by-the-Sea." His mare, a sway-backed piebald, did indeed look sorry beside Vern Bourgly's sleek mount.

"Greetings, Alaric," Ben continued, thumping the young man on the shoulder. He had to reach up to do so. "Were you impatiently awaiting my arrival too?"

"I certainly was." Alaric grinned at the short, brown-haired wizard with the merry eyes.

"How nice to be wanted. Unless — " Ben paused, then thumped his forehead as though struck by a thought — "it was anticipation of our voyage rather than eagerness for my company that caused this impatience."

"We were impatient for both, of course," Morgan said smoothly. "Now, come into the house, Ben, and you too, Master Bourgly. Kerstin, Alaric, please tend to our guests' horses."

The two of them gave the horses a quick rub-down, set out oats and water, and settled them in empty stalls next to Melissa, Morgan's mare. Then they were free to hurry back to the house. They found Morgan and their guests in the octagon chamber, a room reserved for formal occasions and unknown visitors. It reminded Kerstin of the first time she had met Vern Bourgly, when he and Captain Treemount had come to ask for Morgan's help in fighting an Uglessian inspired drought. Morgan had been absent then, gone with Ben Grantwish on their first trip to the Misty Isles, and Kerstin and Alaric had persuaded the men to take them in his stead. Memories flooded her mind like water let loose from a dam: memories of the council in Freybourg, of her fight with Alaric when she discovered that he was to accompany the army of warriors and wizards setting out to fight the Uglessian invaders, while she was supposed to wait in the palace for the returning army. Memories of Uglessia. So many memories.

She shook her head, throwing off the past, in time to hear Morgan ask, "What brings you here, Master Bourgly? Ben said you have a message for my daughter."

"I have," the other replied, and smiled at Kerstin. He was a young man, soberly but richly dressed, with brown hair and a pleasant if undistinguished countenance. "I've been acting as an ambassador of sorts to Uglessia these last two years — working on a treaty, monitoring the situation, handing out payment for *kala* roots."

Kerstin sat forward in her chair, and Alaric's head snapped up.

"Have you seen Yrwith?" Kerstin asked eagerly.

"Yes indeed. I have had many dealings with her. She says to tell you that her land is much greener than it was before you came."

"And is life easier for them?"

"So I'm told. It seems hard and primitive to me," he admitted. "But I gather it's better than it was. Let Yrwith tell you herself, though. I have a letter for you from her. She said it was important, and asked me to deliver it personally."

Kerstin stared at the package he handed her. "Thank you," she murmured, seeing not the grey cloth bag, but a bleak, rocky mountain, a low, one-roomed stone hut, Yrwith's tired face and grey-streaked red hair glowing in the fire-light, her husband and two children seated beside her. Slowly, she opened the bag and pulled out the letter. Yrwith's writing was neat but tiny. She must have worked hard to cramp her message onto the short piece of paper. Kerstin had to peer closely to make out some of the words. As she read, she could almost hear Yrwith speaking in her formal, accented Freyan.

My dear Kerstin,
I hope all is well with you. I have wished many times that I could know how you are doing. I have also wished, many times, that I could thank you for what you have done for Uglessians. Persuading the great ones of Freya to help us has made such a difference. Now, everywhere, I see green among the greys and purples of our mountains.
But I am not writing to thank you, though it gives me much pleasure to do so, but to ask once again for your help.
As you know, I have power for magic, and some knowledge, though my knowledge is haphazard at best. My daughter Redelle and some other young people share this gift. They should be properly trained, but I cannot train them. I know, to my sorrow, what disaster can result when

magic is used by one who knows too little. I wish to send Redelle, and perhaps some others, to your Freyan College of Wizards, but the College only accepts those who already have some knowledge and training. Would you come here, perhaps for a year, and teach these young people what they need to know to be allowed to enter your College? This may be too much, to ask you to leave your family and your own studies. I do so only because I think Uglessia would benefit greatly from magic, if used properly. Also, my family and I would be glad — so glad — to see you again. If, however, you feel you cannot come, I will understand.

Health and happiness to you.

Yrwith

"Is something wrong, Kerstin?" Morgan asked gently.

"Wrong? No . . . Nothing's wrong."

He waited. They all waited.

"Yrwith asked me to go to Uglessia for a year to teach them magic. She wants her daughter and some others to go to the College of Wizards."

Ben nodded. "A good idea. If Yrwith's daughter or any other Uglessian has even a tenth as much natural ability as Yrwith, they should be taught properly, and the College is the right place for that. We don't usually take students after only a year's training, but I think an exception could be made in this case."

"But I can't do it."

"Why not? You may be an apprentice still, but you're more than capable of teaching them the basics of magic."

"But I'm going to the Misty Isles."

"Oh. Yes. I'd forgotten for a moment. Silly of me."

"Would you have to go now? Perhaps you could go when we return," Morgan suggested.

"But that won't be until autumn, will it?"

"No. We plan to leave just before the fall storms begin."

Kerstin looked at Vern Bourgly questioningly.

He shook his head. "By the time you get back and make your way through Freya, snow

31

will have fallen in the high hills, making travel through them difficult, if not impossible."

Kerstin bit her lip. "Could we leave earlier?" she asked her father.

He hesitated, then exchanged a look with Ben and shook his head. "We could," he admitted. "But I'd hate to lose even a few weeks with the Wise Women, learning their magic. I'm afraid your visit to Uglessia will have to wait till next spring."

Vern Bourgly sighed. "I know Yrwith was hoping the training could begin sooner. But if it cannot, it cannot. I'm sure she will be delighted to see you next year."

Kerstin looked down at the letter she held, fingering the sharp edges of the paper. Yrwith would understand. She wouldn't want Kerstin to miss this chance to go to the Misty Isles. Would she?

"I'll go."

Kerstin's head jerked up. She stared at Alaric. "You? But — "

"I know she asked for you. But I can teach them just as well."

"Yes, of course. But — "

"They'll be disappointed not to see you. But you can come next spring, and in the meantime they'll have had a whole year to learn." Alaric's voice was calm, reasonable, almost casual, but his body was as poised as that of a jack-in-the-box ready to spring up when the lid was lifted.

"But — "

"But what?"

"But you're going to the Misty Isles too!"

He was silent for a moment. "Yes. And I'll regret not going there, I know. But ever since you returned from Uglessia, I've wanted to see the land and meet its people myself. Anyway, you'll learn more from the Wise Women than I would. It's more important that you go."

Morgan and Ben exchanged another glance. "That's probably true," Morgan said slowly. "But are you sure you want to do this, Alaric? No great harm will come of delaying the teaching for a year, and you'll miss a unique opportunity."

"I'm sure." There was no doubt in Alaric's voice.

"Perhaps you'd like to think on it for a while," Ben suggested.

Alaric shook his head.

Was he frightened of going to the Misty Isles? Was that it? Kerstin opened her mouth, then closed it again.

"Well, it's your choice, so . . . " Morgan trailed off, and looked at Vern Bourgly. "When did you want to leave?"

"The sooner the better from my point of view. Would the day after tomorrow be too soon?" Bourgly asked.

"That would be fine." Alaric's blue-green eyes looked very blue at that moment. Very bright.

"I think we should think about dinner right now," Morgan said. "We can discuss our different travel plans afterwards." He smiled at Alaric. "You made a good choice," he said softly.

Kerstin stared at the floor. She supposed she should thank Alaric. He had done what she should have done. He was going to Uglessia, leaving her free to travel to the Misty Isles. It was what she wanted, wasn't it? But she didn't feel grateful, not grateful at all. Why did he want to go to Uglessia anyway? Yrwith and her family were her friends, not his. And they had talked so often, planned so long, dreamed so much, she and Alaric, about what they would do on the Misty Isles. Now he wasn't coming.

The shiny bubbles of excitement that had filled her earlier burst, leaving her limp, leaden.

Voyage

Kerstin leaned against the rail, staring down at the white foam that frothed around the ship. When she raised her eyes, she saw nothing but water, stretching like blue-green fields as far as she could see. She had sailed before, but only up and down the coast, never far from land. Now, on the fifth day of the voyage, she felt as though she and the ship were alone in a vast, watery world.

A gust of wind blew drops of water against her face. She wiped the drops away with her finger, then licked the finger. Salt. She should have known better.

She shivered and drew her cloak tighter around herself. It was her warmest cloak, but the open sea was chilly. She thought of going to her cabin, but it was tiny and airless. She stayed on deck, cold but fascinated by the constant but constantly changing sea.

Strange that last week's bustle had ended in this time of stillness and waiting. It had been a chaotic week, with Alaric leaving a few days before their own departure.

She had said farewell to Alaric in the garden, not wanting to go with him to the port. The sun was just peering over the hill. Alaric had stood, holding Melissa's reins, cloak thrown jauntily over his shoulders, eyes sparkling. He's glad to go, Kerstin thought. Glad to go off on his own while I go a different way. She forced her resentment down, forced a smile onto her lips.

"Freyn be with you, Alaric. I hope everything goes well with you. Please give this letter to Yrwith."

He had taken it, then looked at her soberly. "Thank you. I will do my best. And you, Kerstin. May Freyn smile on all you do and fulfil all your hopes and plans."

It had all sounded so solemn that she'd felt an urge to stick out her tongue just to lighten the mood. Instead, she'd smiled again and started to turn away.

Impulsively, Alaric had dropped the reins and reached out to grab Kerstin in a bear hug.

She'd felt her resentment melt away as she returned the hug.

She'd watched them ride away, Alaric on frisky, high-spirited Melissa, Vern Bourgly on his well-disciplined mare, and Morgan, who was accompanying them to the port, on Ben's sorry rented nag. For a moment, she had wanted to go with them, to ride with Alaric through the fields and hills of Freya to Uglessia. Resolutely, she had turned away and resumed preparations for her own imminent departure.

The rest of the week was a busy blur, all except for her two final farewells. The day before they left, she'd gone to the stable and, finding Rainy in the loft, had held the soft grey cat for a long time. Rainy had stayed still, purring loudly as the girl stroked her, rather than springing away as she often did.

The other farewell had been more painful.

She had gone to the peaceful southwest corner of the garden and stood beside the tall pine tree, looking down at the most recent grave in the family cemetery.

"We're going tomorrow, Mother," she had said softly. "We're going to the Misty Isles, just as you dreamed of doing."

She had stood there a long time, breathing in the quiet, pine-scented air. She could almost see her mother's serene face below its crown of fair braids, smiling love and approval.

Now Kerstin sighed, feeling the old, familiar ache, dulled a little with time. How good it would be to have her mother beside her, sharing her hopes and dreams. But Star had died, almost three years ago, of a fever neither Morgan nor Star herself, despite her familiarity with healing herbs, had known how to cure.

The Wise Women of the Misty Isles might have known, though. It was that knowledge that had drawn Morgan to the Isles two years ago, and was drawing him back now, and Kerstin with him. They would learn what they could, so that others would not die needlessly with their lives still to live.

"The air not too cold for you?" A voice broke into Kerstin's thoughts at the same time as a heavy hand landed on her shoulder. Startled, she turned to see the handsome, smiling face of Swain Netter, a sailor she'd noticed before, both because of his fair good looks and because of his habit of staring at her.

"No. I like it." She moved slightly, trying to rid herself of his hand.

Swain tightened his grip. "I would have thought it a mite chilly for a girl like you. Maybe it's the company you like out here." He smiled at her, white teeth gleaming.

"On the contrary, I was enjoying being alone."

"What? A pretty girl likes being alone? We'll have to change that." He drew a little closer.

"Would you please let go of my shoulder." Anger made her voice tremble. She hoped he didn't think the tremor came from fear.

"Why, sure — as soon as you've given me a kiss." His head bent towards hers.

Kerstin took a quick step backwards, but was stopped by the railing. She noticed a couple of sailors standing nearby, watching. One wore a big grin.

"I will not kiss you. Now please let me go." She tried to make her voice cold, commanding. It had no effect.

"Now, now, one little kiss won't hurt you. You might even like it. Next thing you know, you'll be begging me for one." He chuckled and put one hard, muscled arm around her, drawing her closer. His breath smelled of fish and onions.

Kerstin tried to wrench herself free, but her struggles were futile.

"Let me go!" she cried, her voice shrill with anger. Swain only laughed. His head lowered.

How dare he! Did he think, because he was handsome, that she would actually enjoy being kissed against her will? Did he think, because he was stronger, that she was powerless? Well, she wasn't.

With sudden, fierce resolve, Kerstin closed her eyes and muttered a few words.

The world tilted. Spun. For a moment, she felt dizzy. Almost sick. But she was free. Slowly, the world righted itself. She opened her eyes.

Before her on the deck flopped a large, ugly fish whose wide head tapered to a tail that waved helplessly in the air. Its bulging eyes stared frantically at her while its mouth gaped at the air it could not use. Kerstin gazed at it.

A shout brought her attention to the sailors on deck. The man who had been grinning earlier was backing away, eyes wide. The other approached, but cautiously.

Kerstin looked back at the fish, now flopping about more feebly, and decided, a bit reluctantly, that she had better reverse the spell.

She had just begun to do so when others, drawn by the sailor's cry, came hurrying into sight. Morgan, Ben and Captain Merrigale arrived together.

"What's going on here?" the captain demanded.

"She . . . " The sailor approaching Kerstin gestured at her. "She turned Swain into . . . into that." He pointed at the fish.

"Kerstin!" Morgan started towards her, then stopped.

Kerstin glanced at her father's face. Oh, Freyn, he would be angry. Well, she'd have to deal with that later. She returned her attention to the fish and her interrupted spell.

This time, not fuelled by anger, it took longer. Kerstin gritted her teeth and put all her energy into her words and her picture of the tall, blond sailor.

The world tilted again, wavered, then righted itself. Swain Netter stood where the fish had been. His mouth hung open as though still desperately craving breath.

"Hey, Netter, you looked better as a fish," one of the watching sailors called. A roar of laughter went up, breaking the tension.

Swain turned and glared at the other man. "Shut your mouth, Nat Fisher," he growled.

"All right, everyone. The show's over," Captain Merrigale said. "We have a ship to sail, remember? Back to work, all of you. I'll talk to you later, Netter."

They left. Before going, Swain Netter gave Kerstin such a look of mingled fear and hate that she shivered.

"Kerstin, come to my cabin, please. We need to talk."

Kerstin sighed and followed her father below. So did Ben and Captain Merrigale.

"There's not much space," Morgan said, glancing around the small cabin he shared with Ben. He removed a book from a low

43

stool that stood beside the bunk beds. "Please sit down, Kerstin."

She was glad to do so. She didn't trust her trembling legs to hold her upright.

"Tell us what happened," Morgan said quietly.

She did, stumbling a little over her words and keeping her eyes on the rough plank floor.

Captain Merrigale shook his head when she finished. "I was afraid it was something like that. Swain Netter has a bad reputation where women are concerned. Unfortunately, I had to take who I could get. Too many sailors have heard tales of the Misty Isles and won't sail there, no matter what the pay. I had to accept the bottom of the barrel. Oh, they can all sail well enough, and some of them are decent, trustworthy men, but others . . . Well, I am sorry."

"Don't blame yourself. It's not your fault, Captain Merrigale," Kerstin said.

He smiled at her. "It's kind of you to say so, Mistress Speller. And you can obviously handle troublemakers like Netter." His lips twitched.

LINDA SMITH

"Kerstin should have used other means than magic to handle him," Morgan said. His voice was still quiet, but stern disapproval lay in it like sheathed steel.

"I told him to leave me alone and he wouldn't."

"You could have called for help."

"There were other sailors there and they didn't try to stop him. In fact, they seemed to enjoy it."

"We would have heard."

Kerstin said nothing, just looked at him mutinously. Why should she call for help when she could handle the sailor herself?

Morgan sighed. "Kerstin, you know the first law of wizardry is not to use magic to hurt others."

"He wasn't hurt. I turned him back before he could be."

"He suffered no lasting ill effect, true. All the same, it is vital that magic be used to help, not harm."

"It can be used to protect yourself," Kerstin protested.

"Of course. Were you in real danger, though, especially with help nearby?"

45

Kerstin said nothing.

Morgan sighed again. "You have greater power than others because you can use magic. You must not misuse that power. You know that."

"Yes, but — " Kerstin broke off. Swain Netter had used his greater physical power to trap her. Why should she not use a different kind of power to stop him? She didn't advance this argument, though. Morgan might well retort that she could have used a less drastic form of magic to free herself. The truth was, she had been angry. She had enjoyed seeing the sailor helpless.

"I'm sorry," she mumbled.

Morgan's face softened. "Good."

Ben spoke for the first time. "You must admit, it was funny watching him flop about on the deck." He grinned. Kerstin gave him a grateful smile.

Captain Merrigale laughed. "It was indeed." He sobered. "I just hope he doesn't try to take revenge. He doesn't like being laughed at, and he's one to hold a grudge. Still, he's probably too frightened to do anything.

And after I've had a talk with him — which I'd best do now. Please excuse me." He left.

Ben stretched. "I need some fresh sea air. I'll take a brisk walk around the deck."

Father and daughter were left alone in the cabin. Morgan looked at Kerstin's down-turned head. "I'm sorry if I was hard on you, Kerstin. I blame myself. I should never have taught you that transformation spell. It's usually reserved for master wizards with many years' experience. Just because you're so good at magic, and so eager to learn . . . Well, I am sorry I taught it to you."

Right now, Kerstin was sorry too. She was exhausted from the power of the spell, and her head ached fiercely. But she wished he wouldn't blame himself. It made her feel worse, not better.

Morgan continued. "I know this has been a disagreeable experience for you. Believe me, I'm very angry at this Netter. But as your teacher as well as your father, I must make sure you use your power well."

"I know." And she did. All the same, she couldn't help wishing that his first reaction had been as her father, not her teacher.

LANDFALL

Kerstin peered ahead, but saw nothing except the dense fog that enveloped them in a silent white cocoon. Even the men on the ship and the ship itself were only dim, ghostly figures. She shivered, huddling deeper into her cloak.

The atmosphere on board had been tense all day. Everyone had known that they were close to the Isles — and close to the mist that protected them from view. The sky had been so blue and cloudless, though, that it had been difficult to believe they would soon be wrapped in fog. Then, just an hour ago, the first tendrils of mist had reached up, it seemed from the sea itself, and touched them. The tendrils grew. For the last twenty minutes, they had been sailing blindly. Blindly and silently. No one had spoken for the last half hour.

Kerstin glanced sideways, just making out the forms of her father and Ben Grantwish. Ben stood, gripping the rail in fierce concentration. Morgan's lean face and dark hair were obscured by fog, but the taut lines of his tall body showed that he was concentrating just as hard. They were calling, she knew, telling the Wise Women they were coming, asking them to lift the fog.

If their call was heard, and heeded, the ship would land safely. If not . . . If not, Captain Merrigale would have to steer his boat through the fog and hope it would not crash on hidden rocks. He had landed here before, Kerstin reminded herself. Yes. But not without mishap. Not without damage both to his ship and his crew.

How long would it take for the wizards' call to be heard — or for them to realise, with a sickening crunch as the ship struck a rock, that it had not been heard?

Of course their call would be heard. They were two of the best wizards in Freya, after all. But what if the Wise Women decided not to lift the fog? Nonsense. The Women had taught the wizards to mind-call and promised them

49

safe passage at the end of their last visit to the Isles. Why do that if they had not wanted them to land safely?

If only she could join the two men in their silent call. But neither of them could teach her. "It's a way of shaping your mind that I cannot describe in any words that I know," Morgan had said when she first asked him. "To teach us, one of the Wise Women entered our minds and showed us the way. I am unable to do that, or to interpret what she showed us in words." Kerstin understood this inability. But oh, it hurt to be so helpless.

She realised she was holding the railing so tightly that her fingers ached. Carefully, she released her grip.

A low voice muttered behind her, startling her in the stillness. She turned her head and made out the shadowy outline of one of the sailors. She couldn't see his face or hands, but spied the glint of metal held at chest level, and knew the man must be clutching a good luck charm. His words, soft as they were, echoed loudly in the silence. "Freyn save us. Freyn save us." Over and over.

How close were they to land? How close to rocks?

Beside her, Ben gave a deep sigh. She looked at him sharply, and saw his hands loosen their tight grip on the rail. At the same moment, Morgan said, "Ah," softly.

"What? . . . "

"It's all right," Morgan said quietly. "We've been heard. They'll clear the mist away and let us see our way to shore."

"They will? But —" The fog was as thick as ever.

"It will take a little while, but we'll be safe," Morgan said. "I'll go tell Merrigale." He strode off, his tall shape disappearing into the mist.

Ben shook himself. "That was hard work. I've never concentrated so intensely in my life, not even when being examined by the teachers at the College to see whether I was worthy to become one of them. I've got a headache to prove just how hard I worked, too," he added, but his voice was cheerful.

"I hope the Wise Women will show me how to do that," Kerstin said.

"I'm sure they will."

Morgan returned, and the three of them stood along the rail, waiting for the fog to lift. Word spread rapidly among the sailors, and the mood lightened. Kerstin heard talk and even laughter. There was still some scepticism, however.

"I'll believe it when I see it," someone muttered.

A light wind sprang up. Kerstin frowned. She was cold enough already. Then she realised that the wind was blowing the fog away. As it continued, the view gradually cleared, like a glass rubbed free of a layer of dirt by a cleansing hand.

And there, not too far away —

"Land!"

Her cry was taken up by others. A cheer rang out.

Among the cheering, Kerstin heard someone ask, "Do you believe it now, Potter?"

A grunt was the only answer.

"Hey, we're close to shore. Maybe Swain can swim in. As a fish, of course," another sailor called.

Raucous laughter. Swain cursed. Kerstin winced, half wishing she had never turned the man, obnoxious as he was, into a fish.

The boat drew closer, heading towards a small bay, the only level land she could see amidst rocky outcrops and wooded hills. Kerstin shivered. If they were heading towards this treacherous coast, blindfolded by fog . . . But they weren't.

Dark tree-clad hills rose steeply, climbing above the narrow pebbled beach. How different this land was from the rich delta plain that surrounded Frey-by-the-Sea. Strain as she might, Kerstin could see no sign of habitation among the pines and firs. The sun emerged, making the water dance in dappled waves of light and shadow.

"This is certainly a vast improvement over our last landing here," Ben observed.

"It is indeed," Morgan agreed fervently. He smiled at Kerstin. "We didn't realise how close to land we were until we hit the first rock. We were lucky to be within an arrow's flight of this bay, or I doubt we could have limped safely into harbour."

They were very near now, so near they could see the white foam breaking on the beach. There was a flurry of activity as Captain Merrigale ordered the anchor dropped and the rowboats launched. Kerstin waited impatiently for her turn to get into one of the boats. Finally it came, and she was rowed ashore along with the two wizards.

In her excitement, she stumbled getting out. Righting herself quickly, she glanced about.

Except for a small group remaining on board, all the sailors were on shore. Some were dragging the rowboats higher up the beach, but the others clustered together, looking about warily.

"Now what?" one of them demanded.

"Now we wait until we are met," Captain Merrigale answered.

"What if no one comes?"

"Then we camp here until they do."

"What if they — these women who run things here — don't want us on their island?" another sailor asked.

"They treated us well enough in the past when we arrived, unexpected and unwanted. This time they are expecting us. They'll see we're looked after well enough," Merrigale said.

There were a few mutters, but his words seemed to satisfy most of the men. They moved about aimlessly, kicking loose stones, picking up the odd shell. Kerstin shifted her weight from one foot to the other.

"It shouldn't be too much longer," Morgan told her.

"Indeed it shouldn't," Ben said. "Look." He pointed.

Emerging from the trees at the foot of the hill, a line of white-robed women came walking towards them.

The Wise Women

Kerstin watched breathlessly as the women came nearer. She remembered Captain Merrigale's description of them, "coming from the mist, looking as though they were part of the mist themselves." But there was no mist today, and the women looked, as they came closer and closer, sadly ordinary. Kerstin felt a sharp stab of disappointment.

A bird croaked. Kerstin glanced up to see the flutter of black wings as a large raven settled in a nearby pine tree. It croaked again, the harsh cry seeming to mock her disappointment. Kerstin frowned at it, then transferred her attention back to the women.

They were near enough now that she could see their faces. There were nine of them, varying in age from two young women — in their twenties, Kerstin judged — to an elderly woman with sparse white hair. Their skins were brown, darker than most Freyans, and weathered, as though they spent much of their time out of doors. They had dark eyes and, except for the white-haired woman, hair that ranged from mud brown to raven's wing black.

Kerstin examined their faces, anxious for signs of welcome. None of them smiled, but none looked hostile either.

Morgan stepped forward and bowed formally. "We have returned, as you said we might. We thank you for allowing us through the mist." He spoke careful Islandian, the language of the Misty Isles. He, as well as Ben and Captain Merrigale, had learned it during their last stay, and he had taught it to Kerstin.

"You are welcome. You have come, I imagine, to learn more of our skills." The woman who spoke was slight, with an etching of lines around her mouth and eyes and an air of effortless authority.

"We have, if you will be so kind as to share your knowledge with us."

A small smile touched the woman's lips. "If we had not intended to do so, we would not have given you the ability to mind-call. But who is this?" Her eyes rested on Kerstin. The girl felt as though those eyes saw everything, from the smudge on her dress to the questions running around her head. Why had she ever thought this woman looked ordinary? She straightened her shoulders and stood as tall as she could.

"This is my daughter, Kerstin Speller. She is an apprentice wizard and was eager to come with us and learn your arts. Kerstin, meet Amary Ranadotter, who bears the position of Mother in the sisterhood of the Wise Women."

Kerstin was conscious of the eyes of all the women on her. Unable to think of anything to say, she raised her chin and tried not to blush. Amary turned her head slightly and looked at the old woman, who nodded slowly. The younger woman turned back to Kerstin.

"You have magical skills and are here to learn ours?"

Kerstin blinked. The words — only they were not really words, more like thoughts echoing in her mind — had not been spoken out loud. Kerstin shook her head, amazed. A mind had spoken directly to her mind. It had not been what she had thought it would be, not an invasion. More like a hand held out, touching her, linking them. She found herself eager for more.

"There will be more." The thought was amused, but not condescending. It held a smile.

Kerstin blinked again and smiled herself, warmed and welcomed. Then she realised she hadn't answered Amary's question. "I have some knowledge of magic," she said carefully, hoping her Islandian was good enough to convey the depth of her longing. "But that is little — little compared to what you know. I wish, I very much wish, to learn your magic. As much as you can teach me."

"You will." A different voice spoke. It came from a slim woman in early middle age, whose dark hair was twisted in a knot on top of her head. Kerstin glanced at her and started. She looked familiar somehow, as though Kerstin had seen her before. But that was impossible, surely. How? . . . Then she remembered. Her true dream. The kneeling woman in the hut.

The woman smiled at her, and her plain face warmed into beauty. "Welcome, Kerstin. Welcome back, Morgan and Ben."

Morgan gave a small bow. "My thanks." He turned to Kerstin. "Kerstin, this is Rilka Katiradotter. She is the Healer of the community, and was kind enough to share some of her knowledge with us two years ago." He smiled at the woman. She smiled back.

"Indeed, we welcome you," Amary said briskly. "Now, we must make arrangements for your shelter. Captain Merrigale, is it not?"

He stepped forward and bowed. "Mistress Ranadotter."

"What are your plans? Do you and your men wish to stay in Islandia while these three," she nodded at Kerstin and the two wizards, "learn our magic?"

He shook his head. "Much as I would love to learn more about your land, I think it best if we return to Freya now and come back in the autumn to pick them up. Since there is no hole in my boat this time, I plan to leave tomorrow."

"A good decision." Amary made no secret of her relief. "Jaine, will you ensure there is no fog tomorrow morning?"

A stocky young woman with rosy cheeks and smiling brown eyes nodded.

"For tonight, however, you will need a place to sleep. You and your men can sleep in the guest house that you occupied before. We will lead you now to your temporary shelter, if you are ready."

Merrigale nodded and turned to his men, who had been silently watching the white-robed women. He told them about the arrangements. They began to pick up their packs.

Kerstin picked up her bag. As she straightened, she took a final look at the ship. She wouldn't see it again until fall. It felt as though they were being abandoned. But that was silly. No harm would come to them here.

She and the other Freyans followed the Wise Women up the beach towards the trees. Behind her, she heard the flapping of wings and a raucous call. She glanced back and saw the raven take flight, heading inland.

They entered the woods and walked along the shadowed path, dappled green and gold where the sun managed to penetrate the dense growth. Kerstin shivered and drew her cloak tighter, reminded that it was still only early spring. After a short while, though, she opened her cloak. The path led steeply uphill, making her hot as well as tired. She marvelled at the small, frail-looking white-haired woman in front of her, who seemed to be having no trouble at all.

The climb, though steep, was short. As Kerstin reached the summit, she slid her bag onto the ground and gazed below.

The wooded slope led to a valley, set like a gem among the dark encircling hills. A meandering silver stream ran through it, and clumps of hardwood trees dotted the green fields. There were buildings, too, the first she had seen on this island. If only Alaric were there to share the view, life would have seemed perfect at that moment.

Their descent was rapid, and they were soon approaching the stream and the wooden buildings that stood beside it. Kerstin paid little attention to the two long houses that

LINDA SMITH

bordered the cluster of nine round huts. She
eyed the huts and remembered her dream.

Amary led the Freyans into one of the two
long buildings. "This is our guest house," she
explained. "I think you'll find it comfortable
enough. There is extra bedding in the chests.
You may cook and eat in the other long
house."

"Thank Freyn we'll soon be out of here,"
muttered one of the sailors, glancing around
the stark, sparsely furnished interior.

Amary turned to the two wizards. "You
may stay in one of the smaller huts if you wish.
They are usually reserved for the sick who
need Rilka's care, but you may find this
building too large once your companions have
departed."

"We don't want to deprive anyone who is
sick," Morgan protested.

"It is rare that all nine huts are needed.
Rilka goes to those whose ailments are less
serious." The woman smiled faintly. "Rest
assured, we will move you back here quickly
enough should your beds be required."

Kerstin gazed eagerly around the hut they
entered, and nodded in recognition. It was

small and plain, with two low cots, straw mats dotting the dirt floor, and one large window that flooded the room with mellow evening sunlight.

"Our thanks. This will do very nicely," Ben said.

"Will Kerstin be in the hut next to ours?" Morgan asked.

Amary looked at the girl. "If you wish, you may stay with us."

Kerstin gaped at her. Did Amary really mean she could live with the Wise Women, be close to their magic? She opened her mouth to accept, but Morgan forestalled her.

"Thank you. The offer is very kind. Perhaps we could discuss it for a moment."

Amary raised her eyebrows, but all she said was, "Certainly," before leaving the hut.

"I'm not sure you should accept this offer," Morgan said, a small frown creasing his forehead.

Kerstin looked at him, surprised. "Why not? I could learn so much more if I stayed with them."

"I know. And I think they'd treat you well, and we're not far away. But . . . I don't understand. Everything we've learned about the Wise Women indicates they guard their privacy jealously. Why would they let you stay with them? It makes me realise how much we don't know about them. I think it would be best if you decline their offer and stay with us."

A small chill ran up Kerstin's spine. Maybe he was right.

"You're talking nonsense!" Ben exploded. "I'm sorry," he added more quietly. "But when I think about this opportunity . . . I'd give my eye teeth to stay with the Wise Women, but they won't let me because I'm a man. They will let Kerstin, though. It would be a crime to let this chance slip through our fingers."

"What if there's danger for Kerstin?" Morgan demanded.

"Why should there be? They treated us kindly before, when we landed on their shores with a damaged boat, no knowledge of their language, and a crying need to learn their magic. And they seemed pleased to meet Kerstin."

"It's that very pleasure that troubles me. I don't — "

"Master Grantwish is right," Kerstin interrupted. "I'd be furious with myself if I turned down this opportunity. I'll accept her offer, and gladly."

"But Kerstin — "

"You've told me for two years now that the Wise Women are kind and caring. Remember? Why should they wish me ill?"

Morgan hesitated a long time, then asked slowly, "You're sure?" He still wore his troubled frown.

"Yes."

"Very well, then. I doubt there'll be any problems, but if there are, remember we're close at hand."

They emerged from the hut to find Amary talking to the white-haired woman. Kerstin approached them.

"Thank you for your offer. I accept with gratitude."

"Good. We'll be off, then. Are you ready?"

Kerstin nodded and picked up her bag again, glad that she'd packed lightly.

"So you've decided to honour us with your presence after all?" The thought was flung into her mind like the mud balls children hurl at their foes.

Startled, Kerstin glanced at Amary, but the woman had turned away. Nor did the thought feel like Amary's. It was too sharp, too jagged. Kerstin looked around, and saw a raven-haired woman watching her, a faint smile curling her lips.

Kerstin stared back, and noted the tall, lean body, the short black hair, the thin face with its prominent nose and opaque dark eyes. Was the woman angry at her? Laughing at her? The girl flushed and turned to her father and Ben.

"Farewell. I'll see you soon, I'm sure."

"May Freyn be with you," Morgan said soberly.

"Learn a lot," Ben added.

Kerstin followed the white-robed women down the path that ran by the stream, which gurgled quietly to itself. Trees and bushes edged the path, and trodden grass felt soft beneath her feet.

They walked on in the dimming light, the murmur of the stream and the twilight song of birds the only sounds. Kerstin gazed at the white back of the silent figure in front of her, and suddenly felt very alone.

The path left the stream and led through a grove. The trees were tall, wide-limbed, well spread out. Leaves whispered above and around them.

Then they were out of the trees. In the last flaring rays of the setting sun, Kerstin saw a round wooden building, its windows reflecting the sun's red glare.

Amary turned to Kerstin. "Here we are. Home."

THE CIRCLE

Straw rustled beneath Kerstin as she stirred. She frowned. Where was she? Not home. Not the ship . . . Of course! She was in the home of the Wise Women.

She lay still, trying to remember the events of the previous evening. She'd been too hungry and tired to observe much, but she had vague memories of a large circular room, where they'd eaten a simple meal of boiled eggs and bread, and of Amary showing her to this room, where she'd fallen into bed and into sleep.

She opened her eyes and looked around. A pale beam of sunlight lit the small, unadorned room and its whitewashed walls, the bed she lay on, a wooden chest, and a pitcher and basin on top of the chest. That was all, except for her bag which sat in the middle of the floor where she'd dropped it last night. She stretched, then rose.

Dressed, Kerstin left her chamber and looked about. Her room was one of a circle clustering around the central hall, where they'd eaten last night. Though hall was perhaps too grand a name for it, with its comfortable but shabby chairs and couches, its faded circular rug that covered half of the wooden floor, and its unvarnished pine table. No one was in sight. Kerstin hesitated. What should she do? Where should she go?

"You're up, then," a soft voice said behind her.

Kerstin jumped. She turned and saw Rilka.

"I'm sorry. I didn't mean to startle you."

"It's not your fault. Am I . . . Is everyone else up?"

"Yes. We rise at dawn to start our work."

"Oh. I'm sorry. I guess I'm late."

Rilka smiled. "No one expected you to rise early your first morning here, especially since you seemed so tired last night. Nor is it that late. You must be hungry, though. Come to the kitchen and I'll get you something to eat."

Kerstin followed her across the central hall to a large, light-filled kitchen where Rilka dished out a bowl of porridge. "We kept this warm for you."

"Thank you." Kerstin accepted the bowl and sat on a stool to eat. After a few mouthfuls she glanced up at Rilka, a bit shyly.

The woman met her eyes and smiled. "You have questions?"

Questions. She had so many questions. Where to start?

"Why are so many buildings here — this house, the huts for the sick — round?" she blurted out.

"The round buildings represent the Circle."

"The Circle?"

"The Circle. It is the form of our lives. Islandia itself, with its six outer islands making a circle around the three inner ones. Us, the workers of magic in Islandia, who are incomplete unless we are part of the united Circle."

Kerstin stopped eating to consider this. "Do you mean you join together to work your magic?" she asked slowly.

Rilka thought, head tilted to one side. "Not join together. At least, not usually. Not unless the magic is difficult and requires all our wills. It is more that the Circle is always there, holding us, supporting us, giving us strength we can draw on, like the water from an underground spring that never dries up."

"Oh." Kerstin was silent for a moment. "Freyan wizards sometimes join together." The last time they had done so had been two years ago, when she had led them in the spells that ended Freya's drought and sent more rain to Uglessia. "We don't do it very often, though. It's too hard. But our binding doesn't sound much like your Circle."

Rilka nodded. "Your magic is different, I know. You tie yours into the words of a spell. For us, magic flows from within. The weaving feels right and natural."

"The weaving?"

"Evita, the Weaver, weaves our powers and energies together into the Circle."

"Oh," Kerstin said again, though she wasn't sure she really understood. She took another mouthful of porridge.

Rilka laughed. "It is no wonder you are confused. It must seem very strange to you, as strange as your land and your ways seem to us. Come into the hall. Perhaps I can show you."

Kerstin jumped to her feet, still holding her bowl.

Rilka laughed again. "You can finish your breakfast first."

Kerstin did so, then followed Rilka into the hall.

"This is the room where we meet to eat and to talk, both formally and informally, as sisters and friends," Rilka said. She stopped at the edge of the circular rug and regarded it doubtfully. "I had forgotten how faded it is. It was woven many generations ago. But if you look closely, you can make out the different islands that make up Islandia."

Kerstin examined the rug. There were brown threads and grey ones. Dark green and light green. But surrounding and overwhelming the other colours was blue. The blue of the sea, she realised, the sea that lay beyond and between the islands. And the browns and greys and greens must be the islands. Six small outer islands, as Rilka had said, ringing in the three larger ones.

"It *is* a circle."

"Yes," Rilka agreed.

"Where are we?"

Rilka's toe nudged the smallest island. "This is Atua, facing the sea to the east." Threads of grey and dark green predominated, with a line of lighter green weaving through the centre and intertwined greens and blues running into the blue of the sea at one side. Only a short expanse of blue separated it from another, larger island, one composed of various shades of brown and green.

"What island is this?"

"Moria. It is the closest to Atua, and is inhabited by farmers and shepherds and fishers."

"Men *do* live here, then?" Kerstin ventured. "On the other islands?"

Rilka smiled. "Of course. And yes, many of the farmers and shepherds and fishers are men, though women also take part in all of that work."

"But men don't live on Atua, do they?"

"No. Atua is the home of the sisters who make up the Circle. Now, turn to your right. There is another weaving I want you to see."

This weaving hung on the wall. It, too, was circular, but it was not faded. Kerstin was surprised that she hadn't noticed it last night. But then, she had been sitting with her back to it, she remembered, and it had been dim in the hall when she entered it yesterday. Now the room was filled with morning light, making each thread glow with vivid colour. And there were so many colours. It was a wonder they did not jar and confuse the eye. But they didn't. Somehow they all flowed together to make a pattern that was natural, and lovely, and right.

"Evita wove this a few years back, to replace the one that had hung here so long we could scarcely see the true colours," Rilka said.

Kerstin stared at the multitude of threads. "You mean she had to memorise every thread so she could replace it in the exact same order?"

Rilka smiled. "That would have been a feat of memory indeed, though not one, I'm sure, beyond Evita's skills. But no. She knew the pattern of the colours and how they wove together. She recreated the pattern, but did it in her own way."

Kerstin could almost see pictures in the pattern. Almost. Perhaps if she stared hard enough, long enough . . . She shook her head.

"This tapestry shows the Circle, and those of us who make up the Circle. The centre is the Mother, who is all things and from whom all things come."

Like Freyn, Kerstin thought. But — "The Mother? Amary is called the Mother, isn't she? Do you mean — "

"No. Amary is mortal, unlike the Mother who made us. She represents the Mother in our Circle, and the pattern for the Mother is her pattern. Like the Mother, she possesses all the gifts, though none of them are especially strong in her. Her particular gift is the gift of leadership."

Kerstin gazed at the threads that danced and spun in the middle of the tapestry. There were so many colours there, so close together. It was a wonder they did not merge to form a muddy brown. But they didn't.

"From the Mother come the gifts of magic that we in the Circle possess," Rilka said. "Can you see?"

Kerstin could. At least, she could see lines of colour radiating from the centre to eight distinct spots around the circle. Each spot had its own unique shape and colours. Again, she felt that if she only looked hard enough, she could make out pictures.

"Each of those shapes represents one of you?" she ventured at last.

"Yes."

Kerstin stared some more. "One of them has all the colours."

"That is Evita, the Weaver. All the threads come from the Mother. The Weaver takes those threads, and those that come from each of us, and spins us into the Circle."

Kerstin tried to trace the threads that wove in and out, back and forth, from the Weaver to the others. After a few minutes, she felt dizzy. She shook her head again.

"What are the gifts?" she asked instead. "You're the Healer, I know."

"Yes."

Rilka said nothing more. Was she waiting for Kerstin to identify which spot in the tapestry represented her? Was this some kind of test? Kerstin squinted at the weaving, but the patterns baffled her.

Rilka continued, "Gilles, who has a special bond with animals, is the Animal Helper, and Teira is the Plant Helper. Jaine is our Weathermonger, and — "

"That one!" Kerstin said suddenly, stepping forward and pointing to a mass of twirling light and dark blue threads, interspersed with black loops and white threads that overlaid the blue like a thin film of clouds. "That's Jaine!"

"True." Was there a smile in Rilka's voice?

Kerstin felt as though she had just learned the secret behind a puzzling spell. She scanned the other patterns eagerly. One was mostly green and brown, with some yellow threads and small splashes of red and purple. Berries, she decided. "And this would be Teira, the Plant Helper." The one next to it was filled with colours and alive with motion. "This must be the Animal Helper. Who did you say that was?"

"Gilles. You are doing very well."

Maybe. But she still couldn't decide which was the Healer. She frowned.

Rilka went on with her list. "Alannis is our Speaker."

"Speaker? What does she do?"

"She mind-speaks."

Kerstin turned her head away from the tapestry to look at Rilka. "But you all do that, don't you?"

"Yes, a little. Most of us possess a share of all the magical gifts, as well as our own special one. Alannis speaks most clearly and deeply and powerfully, especially to those who are unused to mind-speech."

"Like us, you mean?"

"Like you, and like other Islandians."

"Other Islandians — those not in the Circle — do they possess any magic?"

"Some do, to a greater or lesser extent. But there is only one born in each generation who has the full power of one of the nine gifts, only one who can join our sisterhood."

Kerstin's brow puckered. "Is it always a girl, then, who has the gift?"

"Always."

"That's not the way it is in Freya. Most Freyan wizards are men."

Rilka's eyebrows shot up. "Freyan women do not have magic?"

"Well . . . It's not that they don't have it, so much as that they don't use it. You said we bind our magic into spells, and I suppose we do. To be a wizard, you need to have not just talent, but time, years and years of it, to read and study. And most women are too busy with housework and babies — or are expected to be — to have that much time."

Rilka shook her head. "It is a pity. And strange. But then, much of Freyan magic seems strange to us. We found it difficult to believe, two years ago, that your father and Ben have magic."

"But you agreed to teach them."

"They wanted to learn healing so badly. How could I refuse?"

Kerstin looked at her kind, clear brown eyes and thought that Rilka would have trouble refusing anyone who needed her help.

She turned back to the tapestry. Which of the areas that were left represented Alannis?

The one with golden ovals? The one that seemed filled with the warmth of sunlight and the coolness of water? There was another with

80

brighter, sharper blues and bright, clear reds. Perhaps it was that one. It had force and clarity. But there was another one that possessed a mosaic of coloured threads, each one holding gemlike purity. She needed to know more.

"What are the other nine gifts?" she asked.

"Oh, yes. Evita is the Weaver, as I said. Kirillee is the Singer and the Keeper of our history. She sings our stories and turns our magic into a web of music. Her songs work with Evita's weaving to strengthen the Circle."

"The golden loops!" She was sure of it. Not only did the image make her think of music, the gold strands reached out to the strands that wove in and out of the circle, and intertwined with them.

Rilka smiled and nodded. She brushed a stray strand of hair off her face, then continued.

"Solande is our Dreamer. She may seem old and frail," Rilka added with a swift, tender smile, "but her dreams are powerful. She dreams the patterns of what is and what will be, and who will be the next Wise Women.

81

What she sees in her dreams always comes true."

The tapestry held no more mysteries. "Solande must be represented by the short, clear threads. Which means Alannis is the one with the long blue and red threads, and you're the yellow and blue."

"The warmth and peace of healing. Yes. But I'm surprised you recognised the pattern for Solande so quickly. Most people think of mist-iness, not clarity, when they think of dreams."

Kerstin shook her heads. "Not true dreams. They're very clear."

Rilka raised her eyebrows. "You have true dreams?"

"Sometimes." She almost blurted out that her first true dream had shown her Rilka, kneeling on the dirt floor of a healing hut, healing a man burning with fever, while Morgan watched. But that seemed too . . . too intimate somehow. Drew them too close. She cleared her throat. "Thank you for showing me the tapestry and explaining it to me, Rilka."

"You are most welcome. I know this must seem confusing right now, but I think it will become clear when you come to know us better and can put faces to the names I have given you."

Kerstin frowned suddenly, remembering the black-haired woman who had thrown the mocking question at her yesterday. "Who is the tall, thin woman with black hair?"

"That is Gilles, the Animal Helper."

Gilles. The name rhymed with lilies and began with a soft g. The whole name was soft. It didn't suit the angular woman with the mocking smile. Kerstin made a face. Rilka caught it and looked surprised.

Kerstin flushed. "It's just . . . I don't think she likes me," she mumbled.

Rilka was quiet. "Gilles is . . . a little touchy," she said at last. "She is difficult to know, and does not make friends easily. But she has no reason to dislike you."

That was true, surely. Did Gilles mock everyone, then, whether she liked or disliked them?

"Now, would you like a tour of our house — the Circle, as we call this building as well as our sisterhood?"

Kerstin took a final look at the tapestry on the wall, then nodded and followed Rilka to a long, book-lined room. A woman with dark braids piled on top of her head sat at a table, an open book in front of her, a pen in one hand. Kerstin felt a pang of homesickness for the study at home.

"Blessings, Kirilee."

The woman looked up and smiled. "Blessings, Rilka." Her eyes moved to Kerstin. "Kerstin." Her voice was a husky contralto.

"You are recording the events of yesterday?" Rilka asked.

"Yes. I was too tired last night, so I decided I should do it today before I go to help with the planting."

Rilka nodded. "We won't disturb you." She turned to go. Reluctantly, Kerstin trailed after her out of the library. As she left, she caught a glimpse of the words Kirilee had written at the top of the page.

They came again
the strangers
the men with magic
and with them came a girl

That was all she could see.

The Healer pointed out the various rooms of the Circle. Most were small bedchambers belonging to the different sisters. The two beside Kerstin's were empty.

"Are these your guest rooms?"

"No. We have no guest rooms here. These are where future sisters stay. When one of us is close to death, the girl or woman whom Solande has dreamed will replace her sleeps here while she learns her art."

"But — " Kerstin stared at the other woman.

"But what?"

"What am I doing here then?"

Rilka started and flushed. "You are here as our guest, of course."

"But you just said — "

"Yes, I know, but . . . I shouldn't have said anything."

"Rilka — "

"I'm sorry. I can't say anything more because . . . Well, because I really don't understand. You are here as our guest," she repeated firmly. "Now, come with me and I'll show you the barn and gardens." She turned and walked away.

After a moment, Kerstin followed her slowly. There was a mystery here that she neither liked nor understood. But it was plain that she wasn't about to receive any answers.

Storm

It was good she had slept well last night. She certainly wasn't getting much sleep tonight. Kerstin sighed and turned over once again.

There were too many pictures in her mind. That was the trouble. Pictures of the Circle. Pictures of the gardens and fields that lay beyond it. They danced and swirled in her head just as the threads danced and swirled in the tapestry.

Most of the Wise Women had been toiling in those fields and gardens today. Even elderly Solande had been there, stooping to plant bean seeds.

The gardens and fields stretched out behind the Circle, beside the stream. The smell of fresh earth had been rich in Kerstin's nostrils as she and Rilka walked beside them. Past them, rolling up to the wooded hills, were the meadows where cows and sheep grazed. That was where they had found Gilles.

Rilka might say that Gilles had no reason to dislike her, but Kerstin could not help wondering. The other sisters had looked up from their work to smile and speak kindly, if briefly, to her. But not Gilles. Oh, she had exchanged a few words with Rilka. But all she had given Kerstin was a curt nod.

Kerstin turned over again and opened her eyes. She could see nothing in her room. It was the dark of the moon, and clouds had rolled in that evening, obscuring the stars.

She and Rilka had not helped the others plant vegetables and barley and oats. After a thorough tour that included a visit to the barn, to various sheds, to the beehives, and even to the small mill that stood by the stream at the far end of the fields, Rilka had taken Kerstin to her own domain, the herb garden. Unlike the other gardens, this one nestled close to the Circle, almost under the branches of the Sacred Grove. There, they had planted and tended those plants that produced the herbs Rilka needed in her work as Healer.

It might seem peaceful, this world of the Wise Women, but it required hard work. Very hard work. Kerstin could testify to that. Perhaps that was why she could not sleep. Her muscles ached.

She wasn't lazy. At home, she toiled for hours. But the labour she was used to was reading books of magic and studying spells. Not stooping and crouching, digging and planting.

How had her father and Ben spent their day? Not as strenuously as she had, Kerstin felt sure.

How had Alaric spent his day? He wouldn't be in Uglessia yet. He wouldn't even have reached the hills. He would be riding across the plains with Vern Bourgly. He would be sleeping on the ground under the stars right now.

Kerstin sighed and closed her eyes. She must sleep.

Why had the Wise Women invited her to stay in the Circle, where no one but sisters and sisters-to-be stayed?

No! She must not think of that now. She must sleep. Think of something calm. Think of the sea, spreading like an endless, moving sheet to the place where it met the sky . . . *The water heaved and frothed as though some huge beast strained and reared below its surface. The wind shrieked in pain-edged glee. The ship lolled. Pitched. Slid into a trough. A wave crashed over the side. Another. Men cried out in terror.*

"We must turn the ship!" Captain Merrigale shouted. He could scarcely be heard above the rush of the wind and the crash of the waves. "To the sails! Head west. Go with the wind."

"No!" someone cried. Swain Netter. His fair hair was smeared to his head by the flying spray. "We can't go back there. Not to the Isles!"

"We must. We can't fight this storm."

"They'll kill us!"

"Who will?"

"Those women! They want us to die. That's why they caused this storm."

There was genuine fear in his voice. Genuine conviction. It made the other sailors draw back, glance at him and each other.

"No!" Kerstin shrieked. "They didn't. Don't listen to him!" But they didn't hear her. Of *course they didn't. She had known they wouldn't.*

Captain Merrigale shook his head. "Don't be foolish. They have no reason to want us dead. They mean us well. They gave us clear skies this morning to leave. The storm came up far from their shores."

His words, shouted into the teeth of the gale, did little to reassure. The men didn't move. Then another wave surged over the bows. It swamped the ship, swept one man off his feet. Two others grabbed him before the sea could swallow him.

"Turn the ship!" the captain bellowed.

This time he was obeyed. The men pulled on the ropes. Even Swain Netter pulled. Slowly, slowly, the boom was hauled about. The boat straightened.

"Now bail!"

How long the ship ran before the wind, Kerstin didn't know. She wasn't really there. She knew that. She was in a dream, a true dream. But it felt real. Too real. She shivered with fear and cold as much as the sailors did. She was just as wet. Just as miserable.

Then they had outrun the storm. The wind still blew strong, pushing the boat before it, but it no longer howled and the sea no longer heaved. A sailor approached Captain Merrigale, who was standing beside the helmsman at the wheel.

"How close are we to the Misty Isles?" he asked.

The captain glanced at him. "Hard to tell. We were a fair ways out, but the wind's blown us a long way back."

"If we're close . . . Can we avoid the rocks, do you think?"

Captain Merrigale looked up at the dark, starless sky. "I hope so," he said shortly.

Just then there was a grinding screech, like a nail against slate. Or a rock against boards. The ship shuddered.

Her heart was pounding. Sweat ran down her face.

The ship. It was in danger. It had struck a rock. It might strike more rocks. It might capsize. Men might drown.

She must get help.

She groped her way to the door. Why, *why*, was it so dark?

Perhaps Swain Netter was right. Perhaps the Wise Women did intend harm to the sailors. Why else the storm? Why else the clouds that hid the stars? With her hand on the doorknob, Kerstin paused.

Nonsense. The Wise Women meant no harm. Only someone like Swain Netter would think they did. She turned the knob.

There was light in the hall: women in their nightgowns, holding candles. Solande, her sparse white hair standing on end. A thin woman whom Kerstin thought was Alannis. Amary. Other women, coming quickly.

Kerstin opened her mouth to speak, but Amary spoke first. Her eyes were on Solande. All the women's were.

"What is it, Solande?"

"The Freyan ship. There was a storm that drove it back. Towards us. It hit a rock."

A rustle of alarm greeted her words. It stilled as Amary asked, "Do you know where it is now?"

"Just a little off Atua. To the southeast. Close to land." Solande's voice was thin with age, but she spoke with no hesitation and no doubt.

Solande had dreamed the same dream she had. Help was at hand. Kerstin's body relaxed, then stiffened again when one of the sisters said, on a sharp, in-drawn breath, "The southeast. Where the chain of rocks lies hidden below the water."

There was a small silence. Then the stocky, rosy-cheeked young woman stepped forward. Her cheeks were not rosy now. They were white. "I should have gone further. I should have made sure there were no storms further out to sea."

"No, Jaine," Amary said firmly. "You gave them clear skies and fair weather close to Atua. You did what you could."

Jaine shook her head. "If I hadn't been busy planting . . . "

"Enough. What you must do now is clear their path. Can you make the clouds disappear so they can see their way?"

A touch of colour returned to Jaine's face. "Yes."

"Good. Now come and sit down, all of you, while we decide what is best to do."

Kerstin wasn't sure whether she was included in the invitation, but she moved forward anyway and sat on a couch. A moment later, she realised she was sitting next to Gilles. She edged away.

Amary and Solande put their candles down on low side tables. Amary lit a lamp. In the soft light, Kerstin looked around at the grave faces. They looked alert, despite the late hour and their sudden awakening. And they were powerful. Surely they could do something. Surely they could rescue the ship.

Amary turned to Solande. "You said the ship had hit a rock."

"Yes."

"It will be stuck, then. We will have to turn the tide so the ship can lift off the rock. After that . . . It will have to land so it can be repaired. The question is, can it safely get through the rocks and land on Atua?"

Again, there was silence. Then Kirilee said slowly, "If the Mother is with them . . . " Her voice trailed away. Her hair was no longer in braids on top of her head, but tumbled down her back.

"If Jaine can produce a wind that will blow them back a little, away from the hidden rocks, and the Freyans head northwest, they may be able to land," someone else suggested.

"Even then, it will be risky," another sister said.

"Morn," Gilles said. Everyone looked at her.

"The harbour at Morn is wide, easy to approach, with no hidden rocks," she pointed out.

"It would be further," Amary said doubtfully.

"Not much further. Morn lies on the southern shore of Moria. All the Freyans need do, once they are away from the rocks, is sail due west."

"Yes," Amary said slowly. All around the room, heads nodded. Kerstin let out her breath in a sigh of relief. But then her brow furrowed.

"They won't know they should go there. Nor how to get there. I don't think they even know Moria exists. The only place Captain Merrigale has ever landed is here."

"Alannis will send him a message," Amary said.

"But he doesn't know mind-speech. Only Father and Master Grantwish learned."

Amary smiled at her. "True. But the captain does not need to know how to mind-speak himself, only be able to receive Alannis' message. And she is a very strong mind-speaker, and will have the help of the Circle in her work."

Kerstin looked at the birdlike little woman with hope. But Alannis wore a frown.

"I can send a message," she said. "I can show this Freyan the path. But will he take it? Not only is mind-speech strange to him, he may well not trust us."

Kerstin leaned forward. The edge of the couch bit into the back of her knees. "But he does."

"You are sure?"

"Yes. Why, even tonight, in the middle of the storm, he said the Wise Women meant them well."

Everyone was staring at her. What had she said?

Rilka spoke for the first time. "Kerstin has true dreams too." She smiled faintly at the girl, then sobered again. "Were any of the sailors hurt?"

Kerstin shook her head. So did Solande.

"Good," Amary said briskly. "Enough talk now. We have work to do."

Jaine's head was already bowed. Now the others went still as well. Beside her, Kerstin felt Gilles' body go — what? Not stiff. Not tense. Focused, Kerstin decided. Gathering power into itself.

In Freya there would have been words spoken, the words of a spell. Here there were no words. Only stillness. Quiet. But Kerstin could feel the intensity in the room. Could almost *hear* power humming in the air. And that was the same. Only here she was left out. All she could do was sit. Sit and wait while the silence went on around her.

Not silent anymore, she realised suddenly. A low, almost tuneless chanting had become part of the room. It went on and on.

And there was something else. A smell. A strong smell. Overpowering the scent of beeswax candles, the faint memory of the potato chowder they'd had for dinner. It was . . . Kerstin sniffed again.

The sea. The smell of the sea, here in the room. Kerstin's breath caught. She sat very still.

Then the chanting stopped. The smell vanished. There was a stirring, a rustling. Exhalations of breath. Murmurs. Even low laughter.

"Did Captain Merrigale receive the message?" Amary asked.

"He did," Alannis confirmed. "The captain is clear in his mind on where to go. He was frightened when I first spoke to him, but then he calmed down and listened closely. When he understood there was a safe place to land, he was . . . quite relieved." Her lips twitched at the understatement.

"And the sky is clear now," Jaine announced. "The Freyans should have no trouble getting to Morn and dropping anchor there."

"It will be quite a shock for the people in Morn, waking up to find a foreign ship in their bay," said a tall, straight-backed woman. Kerstin couldn't remember her name.

"The ship will have to remain there some time to be repaired," Solande said soberly.

Kerstin remembered the grating noise of the rock against the ship's hull, and nodded.

"Yes," Amary agreed. She frowned.

Alannis frowned too. "It may be well if I go to Morn. Arrangements will have to be made for the Freyans' accommodation, and mind-speech may come in handy. I will go immediately." She looked down at her night-gown, and her lips twitched again. "That is, almost immediately."

"I'll go too, if I may," Jaine offered. Colour had returned to her face.

"Very well," Amary said. "And thank you both. I think the rest of us should retire. There are still a few hours of sleep before dawn."

Only a few hours? Kerstin shivered, suddenly aware of how chilled she was, and headed towards her room. She was sure she would have no trouble sleeping this time. She only wished her slumbers could last for more than a few hours.

Rilka

The dark earth in front of her brightened. Looking up, Kerstin saw that the sun had finally pierced the early morning mist. It shone on the fresh green leaves of the aspen grove, on the circular house of the sisters, and on the herb garden where she and Rilka were working. The smell of damp earth surrounded her. Kerstin viewed the quiet, peaceful scene with frustration.

She sat back on her heels and inspected the row of seeds she had just planted. Beyond it, the large garden stretched away with its freshly-turned earth and its clumps of plants. Some plants she could identify; others were unknown.

Herbs were important in healing. She knew that. And Rilka had carefully explained the properties of each as she tended it. But in the two weeks since her arrival, Kerstin had done nothing but work in the herb garden. She had expected something more dramatic. More magical.

Not that Rilka was hiding anything from her, Kerstin admitted. The Healer's work in the herb garden had only been interrupted by the household chores she shared with the other sisters, and a couple of visits she had made to the two wizards to show them some herbs and medicines. Kerstin sighed and wondered whether the men were as bored as she was.

A shadow fell on the ground to her left. She looked up and watched a large black bird settle on a tree at the edge of the aspen grove. A raven. Kerstin eyed it thoughtfully. There were many birds on Atua. Birdsong provided a constant backdrop, and gulls wheeled and mewled above the fields. But none were as constant as ravens. There had been a solitary raven sitting on a nearby tree ever since she had arrived.

"Rilka," she called to the woman kneeling in front of a plant a couple of rows over. "Are there many ravens here?"

Rilka's gaze followed Kerstin's pointing finger. "No," she said slowly. "Very few, in fact." A small frown creased her forehead.

Kerstin studied the bird. Wings folded, it sat very still. Could it be the same bird she had seen on the beach, the same that had perched on a tree branch near her, darkly brooding, for the last two weeks? It seemed to watch her, always.

"Your father said a raven was often seen around the healing huts, too," Rilka said. "Perhaps I should speak to Gilles."

"To Gilles? Why?"

"So she can find out why the bird keeps coming here."

"Do you mean she can talk to it?"

"Not talk to it, precisely. But see things through its eyes, and show it things as she sees them. She can do this with most animals."

Kerstin was silent, awed.

Rilka smiled at her. "That magic is more what you expected here, is it not? Not the simple magic of healing herbs."

Kerstin blushed. Was her impatience so obvious?

Rilka laughed. "Do not worry. You will learn more, I promise. But now is the season for planting. And we all learn as much as we can about the materials we work with. For a Healer, that means the herbs that cure the body as well as the body itself."

"I understand that. But . . . Couldn't you hire servants to tend the crops and animals and this garden? I mean, aren't you wasting your valuable time?"

Rilka looked startled. "No one could tend the crops as well as Teira, or look after the animals the way Gilles does. And who knows these herbs as well as I do? They are my friends and grow for me, and I learn from them as I tend them. Besides, we could not have servants within the Circle. Outsiders are not permitted here."

But I am. Why? The uneasy question nibbled at Kerstin's mind again, as it had so often in the last two weeks. She said nothing, however, only returned to her work.

The fragrant herbs reminded Kerstin of the garden at home, and of the hours her mother had spent there, looking after the herbs and flowers she loved. If she were still alive, she would be kneeling there now, her fair head bent over a plant, her strong, capable hands patting the earth around it. If she were alive . . .

"Your mother used to work with herbs, didn't she?" Rilka asked suddenly.

Kerstin looked up, surprised. "Yes. How do you know?" For a moment, she wondered if the woman had read her mind.

"Morgan . . . Your father told me."

Kerstin stared down at her hands. There was no reason why she should resent the fact that her father had talked to Rilka about Star. But she did. Morgan spoke of his dead wife very seldom, even to friends. It still hurt too much. Why to this woman?

"You must both miss her very much," Rilka said gently.

After a moment, Kerstin said, "Yes." They continued working in silence.

Finally, Rilka stood up. "Enough for now. Time to go help prepare lunch."

Kerstin straightened up gratefully. As she stood, the raven croaked and flew up from the tree. She watched it go.

Lunch consisted of soup, cheese and bread. The soup was tasty enough, but Kerstin longed for meat, which the sisters never ate. The door opened. A stocky young woman entered. Behind her came a short, thin, older woman. Jaine and Alannis. Kerstin observed them with interest as they approached Amary and spoke quietly to her. They had been gone longer than she had expected. What news did they bring about the Freyan ship, the Freyan sailors?

Amary rapped gently on the table. Everyone stilled. "Alannis and Jaine have news from Morn," she announced, and nodded to the women.

"You've been gone for some time," Evita commented.

"Yes," Jaine agreed. "We arrived at Morn a short hour after the Freyan ship limped into harbour. It looked like a huge bonfire on the shore, there were so many people and lanterns gathered there. Half the town was up and in turmoil. Naturally enough. They had never even heard of Freyans, much less met any. But they were very willing to help sailors stranded by a storm. The trouble is, the ship was badly gored by the rock. It was only by good sailing and a lot of hard bailing that the Freyans managed to land safely."

Amary frowned. "Will the repairs take long?"

"A good two months at least," Alannis said. "Probably longer, to make sure the boat is truly seaworthy."

Amary's frown deepened. "And the Freyan sailors?"

"They are all settled," Alannis assured her. "But that is why our return was delayed. It would not have taken long to find them temporary shelter, but finding homes willing to take them in for a longer time proved difficult. Nor were the Freyans helpful. They were like a school of fish, unwilling to be separated, one from another."

"You can't really blame them," Jaine said. "They are in a strange land where people speak a language they don't know."

"True. But they wanted the impossible, and were angry when we couldn't produce it."

Annoyance was sharp in Alannis' voice. Kerstin shuffled uneasily in her chair. Not all Freyans were unreasonable. "Captain

Merrigale must have helped settle his men," she protested.

"He did," Alannis agreed. "And Mir and the other town leaders were very helpful as well. Eventually, we found homes for everyone."

"That's good," Amary said, but she was still frowning. She sighed. "It is a shame that the sailors will have to stay in Morn so long. However, everything is arranged as well as it can be. Do you have other news from Moria? Is any help required?"

"All seems well in Morn and the rest of the island," Jaine said. "They are looking forward to Teira's upcoming visit for the planting season, and hoping Gilles will come soon to inspect the young lambs and calves."

She turned to Rilka. "But enough of that. Your help is needed. On our last day in Morn, we were told that a man named Delos had received a nasty cut that festered. Two men helped us bring him here for your healing. It was quite a voyage home. The man kept thrashing about and had to be held down."

"He was so fevered that all my mind-work could do nothing to still him," Alannis said.

Rilka rose. "I will go to him immediately. Come with me, Kerstin."

Kerstin accompanied her to the small shed where dried herbs and medicines were stored, and waited impatiently as the Healer selected various herbs and potions. Finally, she would see the healing magic of the Wise Women at work.

Quickly and in silence, they walked through the aspen grove and along the grassy path. It wasn't long before they came in sight of the circle of small healing huts and the two long guest houses. A familiar figure emerged from one of the huts. Kerstin quickened her pace.

"Father!"

Morgan smiled at her, then turned to Rilka. "You've come about this injured man, I imagine. He's in there." He gestured to the hut behind him. "His arm is badly swollen, and he seems to be burning with fever."

Rilka looked grave. "The trip probably worsened his condition. Still, it was the best and fastest way of getting him help. I just wish they'd brought him to me earlier." She tightened her grip on her basket and entered the building. Kerstin and Morgan followed.

Ben stood close to a low cot. Two strangers huddled against the far wall. Rilka ignored them and went straight to the bed, kneeling beside it.

Kerstin looked at the wounded man and shuddered. His right arm was red and swollen. A long, jagged cut, inflamed and ugly, ran down his forearm.

"I'm glad to see he's quiet," Rilka commented. "Jaine said he was thrashing about during the trip here."

"He — " One of the strangers gestured towards Ben, but didn't look at him. His voice was hoarse. "He did something. Said something. Then Delos lay still."

"A simple quieting spell," Ben explained. "I thought it might be useful."

Rilka threw him a quick smile. "It is." She looked down at the wound again. "Why wasn't he brought here earlier?" Her gentle voice was unusually sharp.

One of the strangers, a thickset man with bushy eyebrows and a sober, dependable air, answered. "None of us knew he was hurt, sister. Delos is a private, stubborn man who hates admitting weakness and has never asked

LINDA SMITH

for help from anybody. He probably thought the hurt would go away if he ignored it. Since he lives alone, no one knew anything was wrong. But when he failed to show up for the fishing for the fifth day in a row, I went to investigate and found him like this."

Rilka sighed and shook her head, looking into her patient's half-open, unfocused eyes.

"Can you help him? You won't have to cut off his arm, will you?" asked the other stranger, a younger, slimmer man. His eyes were fixed on the swollen arm in fascinated horror.

Rilka glanced up and smiled. "It's all right," she said, her voice calm, sure. "With the Mother's help, I can save both his life and his arm."

The Healer bent and took a flask from her basket. "I will give him a drink of spirasap first, to reduce his fever and ease his pain. Spirasap comes from the spira trees that grow on the western shore," she added for the Freyans' benefit. "If someone will raise his head . . . "

Morgan gently lifted the man's grizzled head and Rilka tilted the flask against her patient's lips. A moment later, she removed the flask and Morgan lowered the man's head. Delos closed his eyes.

"He should rest easier now," Rilka said softly. She studied the man for a minute, then placed her hand on his arm, close to the wound. She gazed intently at the purple, puckered flesh, laced with angry red. Then she closed her eyes.

For a long time, nothing seemed to happen. Rilka knelt, her hand on Delos' arm, her body very still. The hut was so silent Kerstin could hear herself breathing. A frown of concentration gathered and deepened on the Healer's face. Then, suddenly, the frown disappeared. Rilka's face softened, yet strengthened at the same time. Her lips parted, and a low, almost tuneless chant came from her. Kerstin stared. The voice, though familiar, was not Rilka's.

Time and place became meaningless. Kerstin stared at the white-robed, singing woman. She noticed nothing else until the older stranger breathed, "Look at Delos."

She did, and saw that the angry red was slowly but definitely receding. It seemed to gather into the wound itself. Then the purplish swelling around the cut disappeared, leaving only the wound itself, a clean, fading scar.

The chanting stopped. For a moment, Rilka remained intent, her whole being concentrated on her patient. Then she relaxed. Her hand left Delos' arm and her shoulders slumped. Head bent, she stayed motionless for a few moments. Then she looked up and smiled.

"He is healed."

"We give you thanks, sister." The older man bowed formally.

"You are most welcome. Much of the thanks for his healing belongs to you, who cared enough to check on him and bring him to me. I would like to keep him here for a few days to make sure his wound is fully healed, and also to give him time to rest. Will you stay here with him?"

The man glanced at his younger companion, then shook his head. "We should return to our fishing nets. We'll go now, and return for Delos in three days time."

"Much thanks he'll give us for our trouble," the younger man muttered. The other shrugged. They bowed respectfully to Rilka, gave Ben a nervous glance, repeated their thanks, and left.

Rilka looked at the injured man, now sleeping peacefully. "Let's leave him to his rest." She picked up her basket and led the Freyans out of the hut. They blinked in the bright afternoon sun.

"You're tired," Morgan said.

Rilka looked surprised, then nodded. "I suppose I am." She sighed and rubbed the back of her neck. "It shouldn't have been so hard, but there was an angry, stubborn part of him that didn't want my help. In the end, I had to draw on the strength of the whole Circle."

"It was Kirilee's voice I heard," Kerstin blurted in sudden recognition. Rilka nodded again.

"Will you teach us to do what you just did?" Kerstin asked. This, after all, was what they had come for.

Rilka hesitated. "I will try," she said slowly. "First you must learn to send your thoughts into another's mind and body. Morgan, Ben, you already know the basics. I can teach you what more you need to know. Now that Alannis is back, I can ask her to teach you mind-speech, Kerstin. Then I can start teaching you healing."

Ben cocked his head to one side. "Am I wrong, or do I detect a note of doubt in your voice?" His own voice was light. Deceptively light, Kerstin thought.

Rilka gazed at the hill in front of them. When her eyes returned to the Freyans, she looked anxious. "I am sure you can learn some of my art. But . . . In Islandia, we believe that only a few, a very few, are born true Healers. It may be different for Freyans: much of your magic is different. I do not know. But I will teach you all that I can. That I promise."

"Thank you. You are very kind," Ben said gravely. His eyes were sober for once. "If you can teach us even a little of what you know and do, it will be a great help, not only for us, but for all Freyans."

Morgan's voice was gentle. "You should rest after such hard work. Can you stay here for a little while and relax before you return? I promise you, we won't bother you with too many questions."

Rilka considered, then smiled. "My herbs can wait. I will be glad to stay here for awhile.

And talking with you and answering your questions does not weary me."

Morgan smiled back. "Good."

Watching them, Kerstin frowned. She turned away and dug her toes into the earth. She suddenly wished they were back in the herb garden.

RAVEN

Kerstin sighed and rubbed her forehead to ease the nagging pain. She felt bruised and battered. Alannis had been working with her for two hours now, for the third day in a row. She had never thought she'd have such trouble learning mind-speech. Oh, she could hear Alannis' voice in her head when the woman spoke directly to her. Anyone could. But to open herself so the Speaker could enter her mind on a deeper level . . . I can't, Kerstin thought. I just can't. I'm too tired.

She looked at Alannis, a birdlike little woman with bright dark eyes and quick, darting movements. Her appearance contradicted her inner voice, which was cool, and clear, and very patient. Kerstin was beginning to hate that patience, which wouldn't let her quit. The Speaker seemed tireless.

"I can't do it."

"Of course you can."

"I can't." Tears of frustration pricked Kerstin's eyes. She blinked to get rid of them. "Anyway, I'm too tired. I can't concentrate any longer."

Alannis studied her. "Perhaps you are concentrating too hard. Relax. Let your mind drift. Think of something calm, pleasant."

Kerstin sighed again. How could she think of anything but this small, enclosed room, the pain in her head, her inability to learn mind-speech? And if she didn't master this first step, she wouldn't be able to learn magic from Rilka or any of the Wise Women.

She wouldn't cry. She *wouldn't*.

"Do not worry. It will come. Relax." Alannis spoke very gently in her mind.

Kerstin closed her eyes. Think of something calm, pleasant. But what? The herb garden was peaceful, but working in it was not exactly pleasant. But perhaps tired muscles were better than her present aching frustration. No. Alannis had said not to think of this. Something pleasant. The sea, green with white-flecked waves close up, dark blue further out. The sea on the other side of the island was a lighter blue. She and Rilka had gone to the western shore a few days ago to gather spirasap, crossing the low mountains to the flat, marshy shore, with its short spira trees and prickly thorn bushes. Kerstin had gazed at the water, wishing she could sail across it and see what lay on the other side.

Dangling willow branches brushed her cheek as she drew the boat higher up the sandy cove. She found a dirt road beyond the willows and started walking down it. Green meadows, dotted with clumps of hardwood trees, stretched towards distant, gently rolling hills. Freshly-dug fields met her eyes. She sniffed, delighting in the smell of newly-turned earth. Seagulls floated lazily above her. And now she could see houses, a hamlet, people coming towards her, smiling. She hastened her steps towards those familiar faces.

Kerstin blinked. Opened her eyes. Saw the whitewashed walls and spartan contents of Alannis' room.

Where had she just been? Where had those pictures come from? They had held the sharpness and immediacy of vivid memories, but she had never seen those fields, those hills, those people before.

She glanced at Alannis and found a faint smile on the woman's face.

"Was that . . . Were those your pictures I saw?"

"Yes."

"But it felt so real, as though I were there, or at least as though I were remembering a place I knew well and loved."

Alannis nodded. "That is how it is when you mind-share."

"You mean . . . That was it? I did it?"

"You did indeed. And now that you have dropped your barriers, the rest should be easy."

"I didn't have any barriers. At least, I didn't think I did."

"Everyone does. It is hard to lower your guard and allow another mind into your private space. Some never can."

"I wasn't the worst, then?"

"By no means."

"Oh." Kerstin absorbed this. She looked at Alannis eagerly, her weariness melting like morning mist in the warmth of the sun. "What do we do now?"

Alannis laughed. "Now we rest. We will start again tomorrow when you are fresh."

"But — "

"No. Don't worry. You'll learn quickly, I'm sure. But you'll learn more quickly if you aren't tired to start with. Anyway, it's still early afternoon. I can put in a few hours in the vegetable garden. Why don't you find Rilka? I'm sure she can use your help." Alannis sounded impatient for the first time, almost as though she were brushing off a bothersome child.

Rebuffed, Kerstin went in search of Rilka. But Rilka was nowhere to be found: not in the house, not in the storage shed, not in the herb garden. Now what?

Just then, Gilles went past on her way from the beehives to the pasture.

"Do you know where Rilka is?" Kerstin asked.

"The healing huts."

"Oh." No patients were there now. Rilka must have gone there to see Morgan and Ben. She had done that a lot lately.

"Is anything wrong?" The words were kind, but Gilles' tone was sharp.

"No. Of course not. I was just wondering what to do."

Gilles shrugged. "Whatever you please." Her tone made it obvious that the girl's actions held as much interest for her as the actions of a flea. Less. She strode off.

Kerstin glared after her, vowing never to speak to the woman again unless she absolutely had to.

What should she do? Work in the herb garden was less than appealing. So were the waiting books in the library, given her headache. Anyway, the library would remind her too much of the study at home, and Alaric. She could go to the healing huts . . . but no. Rilka hadn't invited her.

She could gather more spirasap. It was important work, work Rilka herself should be doing. She had time: supper wouldn't be for another four hours.

After collecting two wooden buckets from the shed, Kerstin headed up the valley towards the encircling hills. The sun was warm on her face, but there was a cool, invigorating breeze.

She walked briskly, swinging her empty buckets, and was soon out of sight of the circular house and the gardens and fields that stretched out behind it. Only the stream, a slender silver thread, could still be seen. She began to whistle a cheerful Freyan marching tune, enjoying her freedom away from the Circle, away from the sisters. It wasn't that she didn't like the sisters. She did — well, all except Gilles. But she was a kindly treated outsider, with them but not of them. It was hard, too, feeling so ignorant. She'd always prided herself on her knowledge and ability in magic. Why had the sisters invited her to live within the Circle, anyway? She frowned, as she always did when confronted with this nagging mystery. Then she shrugged. She'd think about it later. She whistled more loudly until the hills grew steeper and she had to save her breath.

Soon she was descending the hills on the other side, with the low, marshy sea plain before her. Knobbly spira trees spread their twisting arms above tall reeds and bulrushes. The sea rippled with wind and sun. Kerstin gazed at it for a minute before looking back at the curving shoreline. A small object, partly hidden by marsh grass, met her eyes. She squinted against the dazzle of the sun.

It was a small sailboat. Who had sailed across the strait that separated the islands? Was it another patient come seeking Rilka's help? Was she missing something important? Kerstin scowled. Rilka could at least have left a message for her with one of the other sisters.

Well, since she was here rather than at the healing huts where she should be, she had better get to work. Good mood gone, Kerstin hitched up her skirt and waded into the marsh.

Gathering spirasap had seemed easy when Rilka was with her. Today was different. Half an hour after she had started, Kerstin glumly surveyed the sap that barely covered the bottom of her pail, and wondered what she was doing wrong. Was it her technique, or was she tapping a tree that wasn't ready yet? Had Rilka said anything about how to spot the right trees? She couldn't remember.

Croak.

Startled by the harsh call, Kerstin twisted around to spot the raven that she knew would be sitting there, watching her out of beady black eyes. As she moved, her feet slipped. She overbalanced. Teetered. Plop. She sat in the mud at the bottom of the marsh, water up to her waist.

The raven was sitting on a branch of a spira tree, as she had known it would be. Its eyes seemed to gleam with laughter.

Croak.

Mocking her. Made her fall, then laughed at her. Stupid bird, following her around, watching her, spying on her.

She should never have come to the Misty Isles. She hated everything about them. She especially hated this wretched bird.

Blindly, Kerstin reached down. Her fingers clenched on a handful of mud. She packed it into a hard ball and hurled it at the raven.

With a startled squawk and flurry of wings, the bird flew straight up. For a moment, it hovered in the air, a large dark shadow. Then it flew away.

Kerstin watched it go, her rage dying, till only grey ashes were left. What had possessed her to think the bird was mocking her, spying on her? And to throw a mud ball at it . . . She didn't think her missile had hit it. But still . . . There was no excuse.

Shivering, she struggled to her feet and picked up her buckets. She might as well head back and declare the whole afternoon a total waste of time. The sun had disappeared, anyway. By the look of the clouds blowing in from the west, rain wasn't far off. She squelched towards dry ground, her wet skirt as heavy as gem-studded coronation robes.

Once on drier ground, she surveyed herself ruefully. What a mess.

"How dare you?"

The shout jerked Kerstin's head up. Racing down the beach towards her was a boy. He stopped about six feet away from her, black hair dishevelled, dark eyes blazing, fists clenched.

"How dare you hurt my bird?"

SPY

Kerstin stared at the boy, mouth open. "Where did you come from?" she managed at last.

The boy waved an impatient hand up the beach, to where a slight curve in the shoreline hid the view. "Why did you hurt my bird?" he demanded.

"Your bird? That raven belongs to you?"

He snorted. "Of course he doesn't belong to me. But he's my friend. Why did you throw a stone at him? He's done you no harm."

Kerstin flushed. "It was just mud," she protested.

"He says it was a stone."

"Says?" Kerstin gaped again.

It was the boy's turn to flush. His angry gaze shifted away from her.

"What do you mean, 'he says'? Birds can't talk."

"No, of course not. That's not . . . What I meant was — "

"And did your bird tell you that I'd hit him too?" Kerstin continued indignantly. "Because I'll swear my terribly dangerous mud ball missed your precious raven by inches."

"That's no excuse. You meant to hit him."

She was silent.

"So why did you throw your — " The boy paused, then emphasised the next words sarcastically, "mud ball — at him?"

Why? Because she was angry and frustrated and the raven had not only caused her to lose her balance and fall, but had then seemed to mock her with its jeering call. But Kerstin wasn't prepared to admit this.

"Because he's been following me around and spying on me ever since we arrived." As soon as the words were out of her mouth, she realised how silly they sounded.

"A bird? Spy on you? Don't be ridiculous." He laughed, but the laugh sounded false to Kerstin's ears. Hot colour swamped his face.

Why was he blushing? Could her accusation somehow be true? Kerstin stared hard at him, and his eyes shifted again. She frowned.

Even if the bird had been watching her — and why should it? — it couldn't speak and tell this boy what it had seen.

No. Not speak. Not precisely. But hadn't Rilka said Gilles could see pictures in animals' minds and show them images in hers? Could this boy do the same?

She studied the thin flushed face in front of her. The boy's eyes were cast down, long dark lashes half hiding them. His hands, formerly clenched into fists, now gripped each other. Her suspicion crystallised.

"You've been spying on me, haven't you?"

"Don't be silly," he muttered. "You haven't seen me around, have you? How could I be spying on you?"

"Through raven's eyes."

Suddenly, unexpectedly, the boy laughed. "I always see through raven's eyes."

Kerstin didn't see what was so funny. "Why did you do it?" she demanded angrily.

"I didn't say I did anything."

"You said — "

"I said I always see through raven's eyes, and so I do. My name is Raven."

"Oh." The name suited him, with his night-dark hair and eyes and his long, thin nose. He looked vaguely familiar, but she didn't think she had ever seen him before.

Raven was watching her, a gleam of triumph in his eyes. Kerstin was annoyed.

"You *did* send your bird to spy on me," she insisted stubbornly.

"Did I? How could I do that?"

"By seeing me through its eyes."

"Oh?" Raven raised his eyebrows.

"Yes. People can. At least . . . " Gilles could. But Gilles was a Wise Woman with a rare, special gift. Even the other sisters couldn't see as she did. How could this boy, born in a land where men possessed no magic? Kerstin hesitated.

The boy was watching her face. "Yes?" he taunted.

Kerstin changed the subject. "Where do you come from?"

"Over there." He gestured to the sea behind him.

"Moria?"

He nodded.

He must have come in the sailboat. "What are you doing here? Did you bring someone who needs Rilka's help?"

"No."

"Then why are you here?"

"Why shouldn't I be here? I was out fishing and landed on the shore, that's all." He shrugged. "But speaking of being here, why are *you* here? You're a Freyan like the sailors staying with us, aren't you?"

"Yes."

"Why are you on Atua? Why weren't you on the ship with the others?"

"I'm here to learn magic from the Wise Women."

He didn't look surprised. Kerstin suspected that he already knew the answer. After a moment, he asked, his tone casual, "Are you the only Freyan here?"

"No. My father and another wizard, Ben Grantwish, are also here to learn magic."

Again, he didn't look surprised. But he did say flatly, "Men can't learn magic."

"That may be true here, in the Misty Isles — Islandia, I mean. But in Freya both men and women are wizards."

"How can that be?"

Kerstin shrugged. "I don't know. Actually, in Freya most wizards are men. I'm an exception."

"But — " He was interrupted by the beating of wings as the raven flew out of a stand of trees and landed on his shoulder. It perched there, viewing Kerstin from malevolent eyes. The boy reached up an absent-minded hand to stroke its feathers. Kerstin watched, fascinated. She had never seen a creature so obviously wild so content to be touched by a human.

"Are you going to be a Wise Woman?" Raven asked.

Kerstin looked at him, startled. "A Wise Woman? Of course not. I'm not even Islandian."

"But you're staying in the Circle," he pointed out.

"Yes, but I'm only there as a guest." She paused, then added sharply, "How do you know that?" Her suspicion rekindled.

His gaze shifted again. "The Freyan sailors told me."

She considered this. It could be true.

Silence fell between them. In the stillness, Kerstin heard the lapping of waves and the cries of seagulls. It was chilly, standing here in her wet skirt. She glanced up and saw that the clouds had become ominously grey. She bent to pick up her buckets.

"I'd better be going."

"Your buckets aren't very full," Raven observed.

Antagonism, forgotten for a while, flared again. "They'd be a lot fuller if your bird hadn't made me fall."

"From what I saw, they weren't very full even before he startled you."

"From what you saw? So you *were* spying on me through that raven."

A tide of red washed over the thin face. "I wasn't. Why should I spy on you? I just happened to be here at the same time as you were. I couldn't help seeing how slowly you were working. With my own eyes," he added pointedly.

After a moment, Kerstin said reluctantly, "All right." She turned to go.

"Wait," Raven said. She turned back. He fidgeted. "You won't tell them, will you?"

"Tell whom?"

"Them. The Wise Women."

"Tell them what?"

"That I was here. That you thought — you know."

He suddenly seemed younger, a child afraid of a tattling tongue, though Kerstin judged him to be about her age. She relaxed.

"You needn't worry. I won't tell on you."

Her words emerged more scornfully than she had intended. Raven turned red again, this time an angry scarlet.

"You threw that stone — sorry, mud ball — because you didn't want even a bird to see what a fool you looked sitting there in the muddy water."

"You . . . You . . . ," Kerstin spluttered. She tried to find the appropriate name to call him, but her Islandian failed her. "Spy!" she flung at him, and stalked off.

She was halfway down the beach when he called after her, "Why don't you wash your skirt in the sea?"

The suggestion made sense. Kerstin looked down at her mud-encrusted skirt, which was heavy as well as dirty. She hesitated, then set her jaw and walked on.

What a nasty boy that Raven was. Sneaking up on her just so he could mock her efforts at gathering sap. He and that bird were two of a kind. Birds of a feather.

How had he managed to get close enough to watch her without being seen?

Kerstin frowned, picturing the beach in her mind, the flat, marshy land with its reeds and occasional clump of spira trees. Surely he couldn't have crept near enough to spy on her, at least not without crawling through the reeds and getting as muddy as she was.

So he hadn't watched her. Which meant he had seen her through the bird's eyes, as she had originally suspected. And that must mean he had strong magical power. But, as Raven himself had pointed out, men in Islandia did not possess such power.

Kerstin stopped and turned around. A raindrop fell on her head. Then another. Back on the beach, Raven still stood where she had left him. From this distance, he looked small. A small, lonely figure.

She stared at him for a long moment before turning and walking slowly away

THE MOTHER'S DAUGHTERS

Kerstin ate her supper in silence. The sun had come out again following the rain, and evening sunlight made the brown skins around her glow gold. Kerstin studied them, from the lined, parchment-thin face of old Solande, the Dreamer, to the lively face of the youngest, Teira, the Plant Helper.

All, with the possible exception of Gilles, looked content. Tired, but content. I wish I felt the same, Kerstin thought. She had slipped in without being seen and changed out of her wet, muddy clothes, but her thoughts were still back on the beach. Still in turmoil.

Rilka looked positively happy. Why? What had she done that afternoon? As though hearing Kerstin's thought, the Healer leaned towards her. "Alannis told me you did very well today. From now on, you'll make great strides, I'm sure. In a short while, I'll be able to teach all of you how I heal — or, at least, I hope so," she added.

"You could teach Father and Master Grantwish now," Kerstin said sourly.

"But . . . Surely you want to learn at the same time." Rilka could not have sounded more startled had Kerstin said she wanted to dye her hair green.

"I do," Kerstin mumbled, ashamed of her bad mood. "What did you teach them today?" Despite her good intentions, resentment strained her voice.

"How to make that headache powder I showed you yesterday."

So she had missed nothing by not going after Rilka to the healing huts. Looking at the woman's guileless face and kind brown eyes, Kerstin felt small. She gazed down at the table and chewed her lip.

"You know," Rilka said, a frown creasing her forehead, "it's a shame Morgan and Ben have to stay at the healing huts. They could learn so much more if they were here."

She had spoken quietly, but her words came in a lull in the conversation and everyone heard. There were startled gasps, and heads turned her way.

"What in the Mother's name are you saying, Rilka? You're not proposing that these men stay here?" Alannis demanded.

Rilka looked surprised. "No, not stay. Of course not. Only . . . Maybe come to the herb garden each afternoon so I can teach them and Kerstin at the same time. They could learn so much more."

Amary frowned. "This teaching is a burden on your time and energy. I was afraid of that. Perhaps you are taking your duties too seriously and should visit the Freyans less often. No man may go beyond the Sacred Grove. You know that."

"Yes. But . . . It's not only my time that is being wasted by my going back and forth to the healing huts, and teaching the same thing twice. It is their time as well. Morgan has told me that the hardest thing to bear is knowing how little time they have here and how much of it is wasted."

"They should be grateful to you for sparing them any time," snapped Evita, the Weaver.

"They are," Rilka protested. "It's just . . . They want to learn so much. They need to learn. Especially Morgan," she added softly.

Kerstin drew a circle with her finger on the table, not looking at Rilka. She wished the woman wouldn't talk about her father in that tone of voice. Almost . . . tender.

"I know their need is great, Rilka," Amary said, gently but firmly. "That is why I allowed them to return to the islands. But they cannot come here."

"Why?"

"Why?" There was a touch of exasperation in Amary's voice. "Because no man has ever entered the Circle, and the herb garden and medicine shed are within the Circle, beyond the Sacred Grove."

"Just because it has never been done before, does that mean it cannot be done now?" Rilka asked. Kerstin glanced at her, amazed that she was still arguing despite Amary's definite refusal. The Healer's cheeks were flushed, her eyes anxious. "Maybe things have changed. Never before have we met men who possess magic. Never before have we permitted, much less helped, strangers to land on these islands, nor an outsider — " she gave Kerstin a quick, apologetic smile — "to stay within the Circle. Why not allow one more new thing?"

Amary was silent. "I do not believe we should do this," she said finally. "However, this is a decision that should be made by the whole Circle. Should we allow these Freyan men to come to the herb garden and medicine shed?"

Evita's "Absolutely not!" clashed with Jaine's "Why not?"

For the next twenty minutes, the argument went back and forth. Jaine and Teira supported Rilka, while Evita and Alannis argued passionately against the idea. Solande, Kirilee, and Gilles, who watched the debate with a faint, bitter smile, said nothing. Kerstin kept her head down and drew more circles on the table. She should be hoping that Rilka would win. She wasn't.

"I saw them working in the garden," Solande said. Immediately, all talk ceased. Everyone stared at her.

"You saw them? You mean you saw them in a dream?" Amary demanded.

"Yes."

"Why your silence? Why didn't you tell anyone of this dream?"

"There was no need. Since I had seen it, it would come true whether I spoke or not."

"And everyone knows that Solande's dreams are always true and always for the best." Gilles spoke for the first time, a hard edge to her voice. Kerstin's head jerked up. She turned and stared at the woman. Gilles might speak sharply to her, but it was hard to believe she would use that tone on one of her sisters, and that sister gentle, elderly Solande.

The Dreamer did not seem angry, only tired. She looked at the younger woman from her faded eyes and said gently, "My dreams do not always foresee what is best for an individual's happiness. Rather, they show me the pattern of Islandia's future."

"How — "

"Enough," Amary said sternly. Gilles subsided, her face flushed with anger. The other sisters looked uncomfortable.

"If Solande has seen it, so be it," Amary said. "You may tell your Freyan pupils that they may come to the herb garden and medicine

142

shed on afternoons when you are free to teach them, Rilka. I hope . . . As you said, we have already made major changes. One more . . . And it will be good for Kerstin to see more of her father." She smiled kindly at Kerstin.

Kerstin smiled back and tried to feel glad.

After the dinner dishes had been cleared away and the tables pushed back, the sisters sat, reading or talking or sewing. Kerstin asked Rilka quietly, "Why do you think men here don't have magic?"

Evita, her tall, thin body as straight-backed as always, was sitting in the chair next to Rilka's. She overheard and looked up from her book. "Because none of them have ever had enough magic to put in a spoon."

"But why?" Kerstin persisted, the image of two black heads, one belonging to a boy, one to a raven, clear in her mind.

"Why?" Evita raised her eyebrows. "Because that is the way the Mother made things. Kirilee," she called across the room, "would you sing the song of the Beginning Time? Kerstin has never heard it, and it might help her understand Islandia and the Circle as well, of course, as giving us all pleasure."

Murmurs of agreement seconded her request. Kirilee raised her braided dark head from the dress she was mending. She focused her dreamy gaze on the Freyan girl, then looked beyond her, as though gathering words and music from the air. She began to sing.

Her voice was low and husky, pleasant but not beautiful in itself. But it seemed to form shapes and colours, speech and thoughts, till they became more real, more immediate, than the lamplit room and her quiet, attentive audience.

*In the beginning and before the beginning
and forever was the Mother.
From her and out of her she created the
world and all that is in it.
And everything that is, is part of her
sharing in her love and wisdom.
But after she had made the land and
waters and the endless sky above the
plants, the beasts, and the people that
inhabit all her wondrous world she was
tired and wished to rest in a place
uniquely her own.*

*From the sea and the air she created
veils of mist.*

*In the middle of the swirling mist she
formed the nine sacred isles of Islandia:
the rolling plains and gentle hills of Moria
the orchard-dotted land of Tarn, the low,
fertile fields of Lotos and the craggy, hilly
outlying isles: our own Atua, plus Demos,
Kara, Prana, Rork, and Wyth.*

*She created an abundance of all living
creatures for the isles: plants, fish, birds,
beasts, and people.*

*She loved this place, where land, sea and
air are one and so she lingered, even after
she was rested.*

*In those days birds greeted the mornings
with rapture sensing her presence in the
soft air around them.*

*Fish swam and leapt in joy feeling her
hands stroke the cool water.*

*People laughed and loved seeing her image
in every face they met.*

*But the Mother knew her presence was
needed not just here, but everywhere.*

*She could not stay no matter how she
loved the isles.*

*But since she loved them so she wished to
give them special gifts so that when her
feet no longer trod their soil each day and
when her breath no longer brushed the
leaves the land would still be fruitful.
So she made nine daughters from her mind
and heart and essence.
Since they were not the Mother they did
not have the Mother's power.
Creation was not theirs nor could they
spin the fate of lands or people.
The Mother only can do that.
But she bequeathed to each of them a gift,
a gift to help the land and people, plants
and beasts.*

*The sisters did their work and did it well.
The land they tended as the Mother wants
it tended.
As they grew older, though, they realised
that long-lived as they might be they yet
were mortal.
They must have heirs to carry on the
Mother's work.
So they married and had sons and daughters.
Some of their daughters bore the
sacred gifts.*

When the sisters knew the future was
secure they came to Atua where they built
their home and ours, the Circle.
Here they worked and studied and kept
their gifts alive.

As each grew near her time the Dreamer
dreamed the woman who would take her
place who had her gift in full.
That one would leave her home and kin to
join the Circle.

So it has been and is and will be.
In each generation is born one girl who
bears the gift, the gift the Mother gave to
keep her land at peace
to make it thrive
to keep her people well.

The song ended on a note of calm, joyous triumph. Music seemed to dance around them still, lingering in the air. Kerstin blinked, reluctant to let the song go.

"Thank you," she murmured.

"You are very welcome." Kirilee smiled at her and picked up her mending again.

"Does that answer some of your questions?" Alannis asked.

"Yes, thank you." But not, Kerstin thought, the tantalising puzzle of the boy with raven's eyes. She did not mention him: she had made a promise, after all. Instead she asked, "Do you all marry, then, and leave when you have a successor?"

"Very few of us marry and have children," Jaine said. "By the time we reach womanhood, we know — almost all of us know, for the Dreamer has told us — that we will join the Circle eventually, so we don't think of those things. It is our sisters or cousins who bear the daughters who will take our places."

"Why can't you have a family and still practise magic? In Freya, wizards are free to marry if they wish."

"We believe that would both distract us and take away from our power," Amary said.

"I see," Kerstin said, but a frown remained, puckering her forehead.

"Does that seem such a hard life to you, to forsake marriage and children and live with your sisters in the Circle, nurturing your gift and your land?" Teira asked.

"Nooo . . . " And it didn't. Or it shouldn't have. Unlike most girls she knew, Kerstin's dreams had never centred on finding the perfect man, setting up household, raising children. Instead, she had dreamed, always, of becoming the youngest, most powerful wizard ever. So why this hesitation now?

Jaine yawned and got to her feet. "Time for bed."

"Yes indeed." Amary rose and began to douse the lights. The other sisters followed her example. Kerstin's eyes rested for a minute on the tapestry on the wall. It danced with colour just as Kirilee's words had danced with music. The pattern meant more, now she had heard the song. But . . . She frowned. The Circle seemed too enclosed, suddenly. The threads embraced each other but stopped new ones from joining the dance.

She shook her head. She was being fanciful. She was tired, that was all. It had been a long day. An exhausting day.

Two hours later, she turned over in bed for the hundredth time, unable to sleep for the images jostling about in her mind. Think of something else, she commanded herself. Think of home. The old house on Wizard's Hill. Her room high up in the house, with its view of the sea. The study, crammed with books and papers. Alaric, sitting opposite her, looking up from time to time with a quick smile . . .

Alaric. How she missed him.

Suddenly, she was completely awake, staring wide-eyed into the darkness, seeing Alaric as she had never seen him before, this boy-man who had entered her life five years earlier to become her rival, her friend, her almost brother.

But he was not her brother, and the way she felt about him, she realised with a shock of discovery, was not at all sisterly.

And that was why she found the sisters' lives so unsatisfying. She couldn't imagine a life without Alaric in it, beside her, sharing it with her.

It was a long time before she slept.

A HEALER'S ART

"Gilles, when are you planning to go to Moria to inspect the new calves and lambs?" Amary asked.

Gilles looked up from her plate of vegetable stew. "Soon. I still have to go to Demos and Rork."

"Moria has five times as many sheep and cows as both those islands put together," Amary pointed out.

Gilles shrugged. "Very well. I'll go there tomorrow." She returned her attention to her stew. Kerstin, watching her, wondered whether the tension she saw in those stiff shoulders was real or only her overly-sensitive reaction to this woman.

"I should go to Moria too, to check on Delos' arm and to see if anyone is suffering from the spring fever this year," Rilka said. "We could go together."

Gilles flashed her a quick glance, half suspicious, half grateful. "Yes. Very well."

What was that all about? More than simple travel arrangements, Kerstin was sure.

Lunch over, Kerstin and Rilka returned to the herb garden, where they found Morgan and Ben waiting for them, as they had for the last ten days.

"Freyn's Day to you both," Ben greeted them cheerfully. "What part of the garden do you want us to toil in today?"

Rilka shook her head. "No gardening this afternoon. I think you're all ready to learn the beginnings of a healer's inner work."

Kerstin's stomach lurched. This was what she had been waiting for, longing for. But was she ready? Of course she was. She had made rapid progress in mind-speech with Alannis. The work had been hard, but satisfying. And it had kept her from brooding too much about Alaric and how much she missed him. She must be ready.

"We will go to the Sacred Grove," Rilka said. "All important teaching is done in the grove. The peace and holiness the Mother gave it help us learn there."

She led the way towards the whispering trees. The Freyans followed.

Rilka's right, Kerstin thought as she sat cross-legged in the clearing in the centre of the grove. This is the right place to learn. The murmuring of leaves, the distant hum of bees, the green-filtered sunlight splashing on her face eased anxieties, soothed frets, focused her thoughts and senses on the beauty around her.

They sat in silence for a few minutes, facing each other in a small circle. Then Rilka bent her head.

A moment later, Kerstin heard Rilka's warm, gentle voice inside her mind. "Let yourself into my mind. See what I see."

She felt herself drawn in. But instead of seeing pictures in the other's mind, as she had learned to do with Alannis, she saw the Healer's body — not the outer layer of flesh and hair, but the bones and muscles and arteries, the heart and lungs, the nerves and brain.

Time slowed, became meaningless. The wind stirring the leaves became one with the blood circling through Rilka's veins. The grass prickling Kerstin's legs seemed one with the

153

hairs on Rilka's skin, the earth and sun part of the energy she felt — no, saw — flowing through Rilka. All part of one. A whole. So simple, yet so complex. So rich. So right. Dimly, she sensed other minds travelling with hers, and knew that Ben and her father were sharing her experience.

Then the vision faded. Kerstin blinked, and realised that her eyes had been closed. Morgan and Ben wore the same dazed, wondering look that she was sure was on her own face. Rilka sat quietly, with a tired but happy smile. Sunlight gleamed obliquely from the trunks of trees: hours must have passed.

"So that's how the body works, how it feels," Morgan said softly.

"Why didn't you heal the cut on your hand?" Ben demanded.

Rilka looked surprised. "My body is healing it already. Why should I interfere?"

"How would you cure it if you had to?" Kerstin asked.

Rilka laughed. "That is another lesson for another day. You must learn how to see the body as I see it, without my help, before you can learn how to heal it."

"Do you think we can learn?" Kerstin asked anxiously. She had always been so sure of her magical talent. But Rilka had said only a few — a very few — were born healers.

Rilka hesitated. "I do not know how much I can teach you," she said finally. "Your magic is strong, but it is a different kind of magic. I know I can teach you my herb lore, and at least something of my magic." She added, seeing their disappointment, "You will return home better healers."

"Yes, of course," Morgan murmured, his eyes on the ground.

Rilka leaned over and placed her hand on his. "You *will* be a better healer," she insisted.

Morgan looked up and smiled. "Yes, of course," he repeated, but this time he spoke as though he meant it. His hand turned over and gripped hers. She returned his smile.

Kerstin stiffened. The way Morgan was gazing at Rilka reminded her of the way he used to look at Star. But that was ridiculous. Absolutely ridiculous. She was imagining things.

Ben cleared his throat noisily. Glancing at him, Kerstin saw that his eyes, like hers, were fixed on Morgan and Rilka.

"So what comes next?" he asked.

Rilka started and flushed slightly, withdrawing her hand. "You will need much training, of course," she said slowly, thinking out loud. "Unfortunately, I am leaving for Moria tomorrow and will be gone for a few weeks, wasting valuable time. But when I return — "

"Couldn't we go with you?" Morgan asked. "Even if you have no time to teach us while we're there, we can learn a great deal just observing you."

"Yes, please," Kerstin breathed.

Ben leaned forward, his face bright.

The Healer considered a minute, then looked at the three eager faces and smiled. "Why not? I'll have to obtain Amary's permission, of course, but I don't think she'll object."

"Marvellous." Ben jumped to his feet. Kerstin followed his example. As she rose, she noticed a dark form out of the corner of her eye. A moment later, a black shadow flew in front of the sun. She watched it thoughtfully.

Was it the raven? She hadn't seen it since her encounter with the boy on the beach, but she didn't think she'd seen the last of it. Or of the boy. He had come from Moria, she remembered. Would she see him there? She frowned, and walked slowly out of the grove.

MORIA

Moria

Feeling useless, Kerstin watched Gilles and Rilka hoist the sail of the small boat. Gilles had brusquely refused the Freyans' offer of help, and it was obvious the two women needed none.

Tendrils of fog still wove around them, but the sun was shining palely through the early morning mist. She had been awakened in pre-dawn darkness to eat a hasty breakfast, then shoulder the light pack that contained a few clothes and her share of the food they were taking with them. They had met the Freyan wizards on the path and walked through the cool grey morning to the western shore.

Gilles had raised her eyebrows when told the Freyans were coming with them, but said nothing. She seemed preoccupied.

They stepped into the boat and Gilles took the helm, steering straight across the narrow sea that divided the two islands.

Rilka looked at her in surprise. "You're not heading for Morn?"

"Why should I? There are more sheep on the inland farms than near Morn, and they're what I've come for, after all. We can beach the boat on the shore. Do you have any objections?" she demanded as Rilka continued to look at her.

"No," Rilka said, but Kerstin noticed a small crease between her eyebrows.

The trip was a short one, and calm, with only enough wind to keep them moving. Atua's dark hills never disappeared from view, but they grew smaller and smaller as the boat approached the low-lying island of Moria. Kerstin gasped when she saw the sandy beach framed by arching willows.

"What is it?" Rilka asked.

"I've seen this place before. In Alannis' mind."

The Healer nodded. "Alannis knows it well. She comes from a village close by the shore."

"Are you from Moria too?" Morgan asked.

Rilka shook her head. "No." She glanced at Gilles, but the other woman said nothing. Rilka continued, "I come from a long line of fisherfolk who live on Wyth. It and Rork are the westernmost islands, places even steeper and rockier than Atua."

"Do you still have family there?"

"Yes, my mother and two brothers and their families."

"Are you able to see them sometimes?" Morgan asked, his voice concerned.

"Three or four times a year, when I visit the island to tend the sick."

They lowered the sail and hauled the boat further up the beach, then headed for the road that lay beyond the willows. The sun had burned off the fog, and smiled on the tree-dotted fields that stretched out to the low, rolling hills. Kerstin saw a few people in the distance and smelled clover and the richness of freshly-ploughed earth.

How green and fertile Moria was, just like the plains around Frey-by-the-Sea. She could almost see the meadows stretching out beyond the River Frey, the twisting streets and bright houses of the town, the busy marketplace, the dirt track winding its way up Wizard's Hill to the old house at the top. Almost see Alaric, his red-gold hair blowing in the wind . . .

Strange to think there had been a time when she had resented Alaric's presence in her home, had thought him a thief of her father's affection and her own rightful place as the most promising apprentice wizard in Freya. Even stranger to think that she might never have known Alaric if she had not found him, a runaway orphan, sleeping in their stable loft on a spring day five years ago. She and Alaric belonged together.

But Alaric wouldn't be there if she returned home today. He had chosen to go to Uglessia while she came here. Kerstin sighed.

Their progress through Moria was slow but pleasant. They stopped at villages and farmhouses, where Gilles examined livestock and Rilka tended human ailments. The Morians greeted the sisters with joy and the Freyan outlanders with shy but curious courtesy, the adults glancing at them sideways, the children frankly staring before hiding behind their mothers' skirts.

They walked through days of sunshine and gentle rain while the land around them deepened into the green of early summer. Kerstin would have been entirely happy if it hadn't been for her longing for Alaric — and the increasing closeness between her father and Rilka, the meeting of eyes, the laughter bubbling up between them.

Nonsense, she told herself, time after time. They like each other, that's all. But then she'd see Ben eyeing them thoughtfully, and her stomach would knot again.

At first, absorbed in her work, even Gilles seemed content. But as they left the inland hills and descended towards the coastal plain, the woman grew increasingly tense and sharp-edged.

"I wonder how our sailor friends are doing," Ben said as they topped a small hill and viewed the town of Morn at its foot. The town was by far the largest Kerstin had seen in Islandia, with neat, prosperous looking houses of wood and stone surrounding a wide, curving bay. Boats bobbed out at sea and rode at anchor in the harbour, but Kerstin couldn't see the Freyan ship. It must still be under repair. She hoped she wouldn't run into Swain Netter.

Morgan made a face. "Behaving themselves, I hope."

A flap of wings drew Kerstin's attention to a nearby spruce tree in time to see a large black bird take off towards Morn. Her eyes followed it. Would she meet Raven here, as well as Netter? Gilles, she noticed, also watched the bird's flight.

At the outskirts of Morn, a delegation came to meet them. A man stepped forward. He must be the headman. Each Morian town and village, Kerstin had learned, elected a woman or man to lead it for the year.

He was a large, big-boned man with honey brown skin and eyes, and laughter creases around those eyes. He wasn't laughing now, though, as he gave them a formal greeting.

"The Mother's blessings, sisters. We have looked forward to your coming and are glad to welcome you to Morn."

"Blessings, Mir. We are glad to be here," Rilka replied. Gilles said nothing. Mir's eyes flickered to her face, then away.

"I see you have companions."

165

"These are our guests. Mir, please meet Ben Grantwish, Morgan Speller, and Morgan's daughter Kerstin. Ben, Morgan, Kerstin, this is Mir Katirason, the headman of Morn."

"They are Freyans like the sailors staying here?"

"Freyans, yes, but not sailors. They are magicians in their own land, and have come here to learn our magic."

A startled murmur ran through the group, but Mir nodded. "So Captain Merrigale has told me. It is true, then? The men, as well as the girl, have magic?"

"They do. In Freya, it seems, men are born with magic."

More murmurs. One woman even took a step back, as though not wanting to be too close to such uncanny beings.

"Is there much work waiting for us?" Rilka asked.

"A few cases of fever, plus the usual assortment of ills. Gilles," he glanced at her, then away again, "the shepherds and farmers will be happy to see you."

Gilles nodded silently.

"We will stay in the sisters' hut, of course,"
Rilka said. Every town and hamlet had a hut
for visiting sisters: plain, spartan rooms. "But
what about our Freyan guests? I know Morn
must be crowded with Freyan sailors, but —"

"I would be pleased to have them stay with
me and my family." Mir turned to the Freyans
and spoke slowly, to make sure they understood. "I welcome you to Morn and to my
home." He smiled for the first time, the smile
crinkling his eyes and warming his face.

"Thank you. We accept your generous invitation gratefully," Morgan said. Mir's smile
widened at the sound of his fluent Islandian.

"Good. Captain Merrigale, who is also
staying at my house, will be delighted to see
you, I'm sure. Come with me, please. Rilka,
Gilles, I'll see you later."

Rilka turned to Kerstin. "Kerstin, do you
want to stay with us or go with your father?"

"I'll go with Father and Master Grantwish,
if you don't mind," Kerstin said. Gilles had
been too sharp-tongued the last couple of days
to be pleasant company.

"Very well. I'm sure you'll all be very
comfortable with Mir." Rilka smiled at them

and moved off with Gilles as Mir led his guests towards the centre of town.

It was a mild, sunny afternoon, with only a few fleecy clouds drifting lazily through the sky, and many townsfolk were out of doors, scrubbing windows and doorsteps, or standing in clusters talking. They called out cheerful greetings to Mir, and looked at his companions with curiosity. Kerstin heard a few muttered "more Freyans" as they passed.

"Well, well, if it ain't the wizards," a loud voice hailed them in Freyan. Kerstin turned her head and saw a sailor she vaguely remembered stride up to them.

"What are you doing here?" he asked. "Come to repair the ship and let us go home?"

Ben raised his eyebrows. "I thought the ship *was* being repaired."

The man grunted. "It is. Slowly. But you could use magic to mend it as fast as I could snap my fingers."

"Sorry," Ben said. "Wizards don't use magic to do tasks that hands and hard work can do better. We're just here for a visit."

The man scowled. "So we're stuck here for another few months."

"Don't you like it here?"

The sailor shrugged. "It's not bad, but I get tired of hearing all this foreign jabber. Mind you, the girls are pretty." He leered. Kerstin remembered him now. He was the man who stood by grinning when Swain Netter tried to kiss her.

Morgan frowned. "I trust you're keeping out of trouble," he said sharply.

"Not to worry. I can look after myself. Anyway, old Merrigale keeps his eagle eyes on us. Well, see you around." He swaggered off. Kerstin watched him go. She noticed that Mir also looked after him, grim-faced.

Their way led towards the waterfront. As they approached the sea, Kerstin took deep breaths of the fishy, salty air, which reminded her of home.

Mir stopped in front of a two-storied wooden house with gable windows over-looking the bay. "Here we are," he announced, opening the door. The smell of freshly-baked bread greeted them.

"Mirra!" he called.

A girl who looked a couple of years older than Kerstin entered from the back room. A tall, big-boned girl with smooth brown hair and large, beautiful brown eyes, she bore a strong resemblance to Mir. Despite her size, she moved with grace.

"This is my daughter," Mir said unnecessarily. "Mirra, meet our new guests. They will be staying with us for a few days. This is Ben Grantwish, Morgan Speller, and his daughter Kerstin. They come from Freya."

"Freya? There's another ship come from Freya?" Alarm made Mirra's voice high.

Ben smiled at her. "No more Freyans, I promise you. We arrived on the last ship, and have been staying with the Wise Women on Atua. We came to Moria with a couple of sisters to see your lovely island."

"A couple of sisters?" Mirra echoed. She glanced at her father. "Did . . . Who came here?"

Mir looked at her steadily. "Rilka and Gilles."

Mirra said nothing, but her eyes widened and blood drained from her face. Kerstin remembered how Mir had looked at Gilles, then looked away.

The uncomfortable silence was broken by Mir. "Where's Captain Merrigale? He'll want to see our guests."

"Captain Merrigale?" Mirra repeated. "He went out. To check on some of his men, I think. He said he'd be back for dinner."

"Have the sailors been giving you trouble?" Ben asked.

Mir shrugged. "A few have been . . . annoying, shall we say? But Captain Merrigale is good at keeping his eye on them, and most have proved courteous enough, and have even helped with mending nets and fishing. Come, I'll show you your rooms."

Kerstin was to sleep on a mat in Mirra's room, while her father and Ben would share the chamber Captain Merrigale was using. Alone in her room, Kerstin looked out the gable window to the sea beyond, glittering in the late afternoon sun. The breeze blowing in through the open window was warm, and the scene before her peaceful, but Kerstin felt as jittery as though she were walking on ground that held hidden rocks and unseen quicksand.

Croak.

Kerstin turned her head quickly and saw the familiar bird perched on the roof.

"I might have known you'd be here, you croaking spy," she told it. Its black eyes watched her, unblinking. "Where you are, there's sure to be trouble."

MIRRA

As Kerstin was descending the stairs, Captain Merrigale opened the door and came in. He stopped in surprise.

"Mistress Speller! What brings you here?"

"We — Father, Master Grantwish and I — are visiting Moria with two Wise Women."

"Will you be here long?"

Kerstin shook her head. "A few days only."

"Not long enough. Still, it will be good to have your company while you're here — and good to talk over a few things."

Morgan, who had come to the doorway between the parlour and hall, heard this. "Problems?" he asked.

"Morgan! Glad to see you. As to problems — well, there are some, though none so far that I can't handle with Mir's help. He's very good at soothing his people's ruffled feathers when my sailors get on their nerves — which they do, Freyn's curse on them. Oh, most of the men are fine. They work hard at the ship repairs, go fishing with their hosts, help mend the nets, even try to learn the language. But others! . . . Nothing but grumble and complain. Won't do a stitch of work, just lounge around all day, sneering at the townsfolk and drinking the local beer. Feel they're badly done by if they don't get enough of it."

"You can't make them work on the repairs?"

Merrigale grimaced. "I tried that. To be honest, they did such shoddy work I stopped insisting. They were really annoying the boat builders in Mir's shop, who take pride in their work. I was glad to see their backs — except that it left them with too much idle time on their hands."

"I imagine our friend Netter's one of the worst," Morgan said.

"Surprisingly enough, no. Oh, he's not helping with the ship. But he does go out fishing with the men here and has become quite chummy with some of them. He's even learned a fair bit of Islandian. A changed man, Netter."

LINDA SMITH

Kerstin doubted it.

"Anyway," the captain continued, "we'll manage. Unless some hothead starts a fight, that is."

"How are the repairs to the ship coming along?"

"Slower than I'd hoped," Merrigale admitted. "As I said, the boat builders here are good. They've discovered a few flaws in the ship that should be seen to before we set sail again. All this means it will take another couple of months before we can go. By that time, it will be getting so close to your intended date of departure that we may as well stay till you're ready to leave."

Ben came down the stairs then to exchange greetings with Merrigale, and the three men entered the parlour. Kerstin trailed after them into the comfortably furnished room with its stone fireplace and large window looking out on the harbour.

"Dinner will be ready soon," Mir told them. Kerstin sniffed hungrily. Roast lamb. It felt like ages since she'd eaten meat.

The door opened and closed quietly behind her.

"There you are," Mir said, a touch of annoyance in his voice. "Just in time for dinner."

Kerstin turned.

The thin, black-haired boy who had just entered stopped. His face turned tomato red. It was Raven.

Kerstin heard little as Mir introduced his son. Raven mumbled his greetings and didn't look at her again. In fact, he scarcely looked at anyone. He had gone from red to white.

Kerstin found it hard to concentrate on the meal, tasty as it was. The adults talked easily enough, though Kerstin thought Mir seemed absent-minded at times. But the young people ate in silence, except once when Mirra leaned over to her brother and asked in a low voice, "Do you know — "

"Yes."

Neither said more. They continued to pick at their food. Kerstin watched them from under her lashes and sighed. She was not looking forward to sharing a room with Mirra. As for Raven . . . She glanced at him and saw that he was looking at her. He averted his gaze. She sighed again.

When the meal ended, Mirra and Raven disappeared into the kitchen to do the washing up.

Kerstin sat in the parlour, half listening to the men's conversation. After a while, she excused herself to go to her room.

Raven was lurking in the hall.

"Uh . . . Kerstin . . ."

She waited.

"You won't say anything, will you? To Father?"

"Say anything?" She raised her eyebrows. "About what?"

He fidgeted. "About . . . you know. Meeting me on Atua. What you thought."

"I thought you were spying on me. I still do."

"I wasn't. At least . . . "

She said nothing.

Raven hesitated, then looked directly at her. His eyes were bright. "Look, Father has enough — more than enough — to worry about. He doesn't need this."

Kerstin raised her eyebrows again. "Are you saying it's him you're trying to protect, not yourself?"

Raven flushed scarlet. He glared at her, then turned and stalked away.

"Wait," Kerstin called, but he didn't stop. A moment later the front door banged behind him. Kerstin bit her lip, regretting her words. She shouldn't have sounded so scornful, even if she *had* doubted him. At least she could have told him she'd hold her tongue.

Tomorrow, she promised herself as she trudged upstairs. I'll tell him tomorrow. If he lets me, that is.

She hoped their stay in Morn would be brief.

She was dreaming. She knew she was dreaming, and that it was a true dream. All the same, she couldn't help crying out in joyous surprise, "Alaric!"

He paid no attention. He was scrambling up a rocky grey cliff, searching for handholds and toeholds with some difficulty. She held her breath as he fumbled for the next hold. Then he found it, and the next, and swung himself up onto a small plateau. From there, he surveyed the world below.

Kerstin, an invisible presence, viewed it with him. Far below stood Yrwith's and Bron's small stone hut. Ursells, grey, sure-footed animals that seemed half goat, half horse, climbed up the mountain. There were green patches, she noted with a fierce rush of pride, and a rivulet rushing through a crack in the rocks.

A shout came from behind them. Alaric turned.

Running towards him, red hair flying, was Yrwith's daughter Redelle. Laughing, she flung her arms around him.

"You did it! You climbed the mountain all by yourself!"

"I said I would."

They hugged each other exuberantly. Then they sobered and stood with their arms around each other, gazing at one another.

"Alaric," Kerstin said. Pleaded. But of course he didn't hear her.

Alaric and Redelle stood motionless, regarding each other gravely, while the wind sighed around them and a hawk circled over-head. Then Redelle released herself gently and took his hand. "Come. Let's go home." They headed for an easier, more gradual path down the mountain.

Kerstin stood for a long time watching them get smaller and smaller, till everything disappeared in a swirl of mist.

She awoke with tears on her face. For a moment she stared, bewildered, into the grey morning light. Where was she? Where were Alaric and Redelle and the mountains of Uglessia? Then she remembered and turned over with a muffled groan.

She was in Morn, on Moria, in Islandia, far away from Alaric and Uglessia. She couldn't leave till fall. Even then, she wouldn't be able to go to him, not with winter snow blocking the mountains. She would have to wait till spring to see him, to make him look at her the way he had looked at Redelle.

Didn't Alaric know they belonged together? When she'd realised she loved him, it had seemed so right, so inevitable. She'd been sure he must feel the same. Now . . . A sob wrenched her.

"What is it? What's wrong?"

Kerstin stiffened. She clenched her throat and scrubbed at her eyes. She turned her head and looked at Mirra. The older girl was sitting up in bed, her brown eyes worried.

"What is it?" she repeated. "Are you hurt?"

"No," Kerstin muttered. After a pause, she added, "It was a dream."

"Oh." Mirra sounded relieved. "Just a dream." She laughed and lay back down.

"It wasn't just a dream," Kerstin protested. "It was a true dream."

"A true dream?"

"I dream them sometimes. They're real." How she wished this one wasn't.

Mirra laughed again, but this time it was a strangled, bitter laugh. "Oh yes. Real. Just like the dreams of the Wise Women. How can you think your dreams speak the truth?"

"Because they do."

"They're lies. Nothing but lies, do you hear me?" Mirra was sitting up again, but now her voice, her whole body, was shaking with rage.

"But — "

"And if they are true, if the Wise Women dream truly but say . . . say . . . then they're cruel and I hate them!"

181

"Cruel? Who? What? The dreams, you mean? But — "

"The Wise Women. You're staying with them, aren't you? How can you stand it? Or don't you care? I hate them!" Mirra was out of bed now, on her feet. For a minute she stood, glaring at Kerstin as though she hated her too. Then she whirled and ran out of the room, nightgown flapping. Kerstin heard her bare feet pound down the stairs. A moment later, the front door opened, then slammed shut.

Was everyone in this house mad? Kerstin sat up, ready to race after Mirra. Then she lay down again. Why should she? Mirra didn't want her. No one wanted her. Alaric . . . Another sob rose in her throat. She stifled it.

Why had Mirra said the Wise Women were cruel? Why did she mistrust their dreams?

Why had the Wise Women invited Kerstin to live in the Circle with them? She had never understood that.

For a moment she lay there, biting her lip. Then, slowly, she rose, pulled a dress over her nightgown, tugged on her boots. She would follow Mirra after all. She needed some answers.

INHERITANCE

Emerging from the house, Kerstin realised just how early it was. The streets were deserted and the sky a pale, thin blue. Luckily there was no fog this morning. But where had Mirra gone? Kerstin peered in all directions but could see no sign of her.

If *she* were angry and distressed, she would have gone down to the shore for refuge. Kerstin headed in that direction.

She heard Mirra before she saw her. Desolate sobs came from behind a rock. Kerstin stopped, then took a backwards step. She'd hate it if someone she barely knew intruded on her private grief.

Then she heard a voice she knew. "What's a pretty girl like you doing crying?"

The sobs broke off.

"Need a bit of comforting, do you? Nothing like a kiss and a cuddle to cheer you up, I always say. Why, you're even dressed for it, in your nightie and all." A chuckle.

Swain Netter.

"Go away." Mirra's voice was stern, commanding, all trace of tears gone from it, but it had no effect.

"You don't mean that. Come on, now. We're all alone here."

"I said, go away."

Netter laughed.

Kerstin hesitated no longer. She stepped out from behind the rock.

"Don't worry about him, Mirra. Just turn him into a fish. It suits him. There's even a lot of water for him to swim in." She gestured to the sea beyond them.

The others turned to stare at her. Mirra, her face tear-stained, looked pale but determined. She held a rock in her hand. Netter scowled at Kerstin. He took a threatening step towards her, then hesitated.

"What type of fish would you like to be this time, Master Netter?" Kerstin taunted.

For a long moment he stood there, his handsome face torn between rage and fear. Fear won.

"Freyn's curse on you and all magicking women," he snarled. He turned and stomped away.

Kerstin felt limp with relief but didn't let it show until he was out of sight. Then she sank onto the rocky sand. Mirra remained standing, but let the rock drop.

"I suppose you think I should thank you," she said coldly.

Kerstin did, but didn't say so.

"Well, I'm not going to. I didn't ask for your help. I can look after myself. I don't need someone with magic."

Kerstin felt too tired to respond, even to get angry.

"I suppose you think you're better than I am because you can use magic. Well, you're not. And if you hadn't come here in the first place to learn more magic, horrid men like him wouldn't even be here." Mirra paused, but Kerstin still said nothing.

"I don't care if you have magic or not. Live with the Wise Women if you want. Just leave me and my family alone." With an angry sniff, Mirra turned and walked away.

"Wait."

Mirra kept walking.

"Wait!" Kerstin pulled herself to her feet and started after the other girl. Mirra broke into a stumbling run. Kerstin caught up with her and tugged at her arm.

"Mirra — "

"Leave me alone!"

Kerstin felt a revitalising flash of anger. "I will leave you alone. I'll be glad to leave you alone. You and all your family. It's you — or your brother, anyway — who won't leave me alone."

Mirra stared at her blankly. "What are you talking about?"

Kerstin ignored the question. "But you can't tell me that you hate the Wise Women, that they're cruel, and not tell me why. I'm living with them, after all."

Mirra looked at her mutely. Kerstin wanted to shake her. Instead, she forced herself to drop her hand and say quietly, "Please."

After a moment, Mirra covered her face with her hands. "Oh, Mother." She was silent for a couple of heartbeats. "All right." She dropped her hands. "I'll tell you. But it will take a while."

"Let's sit down, then."

There was a log a few feet away. Kerstin walked to it, turning her head a couple of times to make sure Mirra was following her. As she reached it, she noticed a small, spiny round shape on it and started to brush it away.

"No!" Mirra grabbed her arm so quickly that Kerstin lost her balance and fell to her knees. A sharp rock dug into her flesh. She looked up angrily.

"What was that all about?"

Mirra was white. "That was a spinella, a small sea creature. They don't usually come onto land."

Kerstin stared at her. "So?"

"They — spinellas — are very poisonous. If you'd put your hand on it . . . " Mirra shuddered.

Kerstin swallowed. "What would have happened?"

"There is no antidote. Within an hour, you'd be dead. At least . . . maybe not." She looked away. "Not with Rilka here. She could probably save you, though even she couldn't save the boy last year. But I suppose it was too late by the time they got him to her. He was only four," she added.

Kerstin swallowed again. "Thank you." Her voice was hoarse. She cleared it. "Thank you for saving my life."

Mirra glanced back at her. For the first time that day, a smile flickered across her face. "Thank you for saving me from that man."

"Or from having to clonk him on the head with that rock you were holding?"

Mirra's smile broadened. "Or from that," she agreed. Her smile faded. "If you still want to hear my story, we should find a better place to sit."

Kerstin glanced again at the small, innocent-looking spinella, and scrambled to her feet, keeping well back from the log. They found a safe, if slightly damp log closer to the water's edge and sat, facing the sea. Mirra watched the incoming tide for a while, then took a deep breath.

"When my parents were young, they liked each other. But before marrying, or even allowing themselves to feel too much for one another, they consulted Solande, the Dreamer. Mother's family possesses one of the nine gifts, and Mother herself had great potential. They thought she might be chosen to join the Circle. But the sister who had the same gift as Mother was not old. It was also possible that her successor would be Mother's daughter, or a niece, or a cousin's daughter. So they asked Solande, who is supposed to know these things, if they should marry. Solande had one of her 'true dreams' and said yes. So they married, and were happy. For fifteen years they were happy."

She fell silent. Kerstin waited.

"Then the sister died in a sudden, freak accident and Solande had another dream. Mother was called to the Circle."

Pictures slid together in Kerstin's mind, like a puzzle solving itself. "Gilles," she breathed.

Everything fit: the way Mir avoided looking at Gilles, the way Mirra reacted to news of the sisters' presence in Morn, even Gilles' bitterness. And Raven, she realised suddenly, bore a striking resemblance to Gilles.

Mirra nodded.

"She couldn't refuse?"

"No one refuses."

"But Solande — none of the Wise Women — would lie to your parents. They wouldn't play a cruel trick like that. They're not heartless."

"No? What then? Are the dreams false?"

Kerstin was silent.

After a moment, Mirra continued with difficulty. "There is only one reason I can think of for Solande's dreams. Magic runs very strongly in both Mother's and Father's families. Father is Rilka's second cousin, you know, and even though a gift can't be handed down through him, his blood could strengthen his daughter's magic. If I had inherited strong magical powers, then my parents' marriage would have served Islandia well. But I didn't inherit anything. I have no magic. No magic at all."

"Mirra — "

"I thought, when Mother was called . . . Often the gift doesn't appear until adolescence. I was fourteen when Mother was called, and Raven eleven. I was a late developer. I thought that if I had a gift it might make their pain, if not worthwhile, at least more bearable. I've watched Father . . . Oh, he keeps busy, first with his boat building business, and now with town affairs, but . . . They were very much in love. It hurt them so. It hurt *us* so," she corrected herself softly.

"And then I entered womanhood, and showed no talent for magic whatsoever. The only talents I have are for cooking and boat building," she concluded bitterly.

The sun had risen. Kerstin scowled at the glory of the pink and gold sky and tried to think of words she could say. She found none. All she had was a question. "Isn't she . . . Even if she must live on Atua, why can't she visit you? Why can't she stay with you when she comes to Morn? Is it forbidden?"

"No." Mirra was silent a minute, staring out to sea. "She can visit. She can stay. She has. But it hurt too much, knowing she must leave. Hurt all of us, but especially her. Now, when she comes — and she comes very seldom — she avoids us as much as possible."

Down the beach, men and women were preparing their fishing boats. Mirra stirred. "I suppose we should go home before anyone else catches me in my nightgown."

They headed back. Before they reached the house, Mirra turned to Kerstin. "You won't say anything, will you? About my losing my temper, or the meeting with that man, or my telling you our story?"

This family was always asking her to keep secrets. First Raven. Now Mirra.

Raven. She frowned thoughtfully.

"Mirra," she said slowly, "I know it's thought that only women have magic in Islandia. But is it possible . . . You said that both branches of your family have strong magical talent. Could Raven have inherited one of the magical gifts? If so, that would explain Solande's dreams."

Mirra was shaking her head. "No. I'd know if he had. Raven may be different than other boys in some ways, but he's not *that* different. Anyway, it's impossible. But do you promise not to tell anyone? Especially Father. Or Mother," she added in a low voice.

"Yes, of course."

She followed Mirra into the house, still frowning.

FIFTH WHEEL

They were sitting over the remains of breakfast when a knock came at the front door. Raven went to answer it. He'd been silent throughout the meal, as had Mirra, but he'd kept darting glances at his sister. When the two girls had entered the house earlier that morning, Raven had been descending the stairs. The look of shocked amazement on his face when he saw Mirra in her nightgown had almost made Kerstin giggle.

"Blessings, Raven," they heard a bass voice say. "Is your father at home?"

"Graf! Come in," Mir called, and stood to greet his visitor, a short, stocky man with a mop of curly hair. "We're just finishing breakfast. Won't you join us?"

Graf shook his head. "I'm afraid I'm on business that won't wait. There's a fight going on between some of our men and the Freyans."

Mir frowned. "Serious?"

Graf shrugged. "They're just trading punches at the moment. No one's drawn a knife yet. But the fight seems to be spreading."

"How did it start?" Captain Merrigale asked.

The newcomer shrugged again. "I don't know exactly. I heard that Griffin told one of the Freyans that he could help, not just lounge around watching the fishers prepare their boats. Either the Freyan didn't like Griffin's tone, or Griffin didn't like his answer. Whichever way, they started fighting. Then others joined in on both sides."

"Freyn's curse on them!" Merrigale swore. "I've warned my men I don't know how many times."

"The blame is not all your men's. This is not the way to treat guests," Mir said sternly. "Come, Captain, we shall settle this matter."

Ben stood up. "I'll go with you. Coming, Morgan?"

Morgan hesitated, then shook his head. "I'll stay here."

Mir glanced at his children. "You'll look after our guests?"

"I thought . . . There are things I should see to at the shop," Mirra said.

Mir nodded. "Very well. Mirra has run our boat building business ever since I was chosen headman," he told the Freyans, giving his daughter a warm smile. Look, Mirra, Kerstin urged silently. See how proud your father is of you. It doesn't matter that you don't have magic.

"Raven," Mir ordered his son, "make sure our guests are cared for."

Raven nodded.

After the others departed, Morgan disappeared into the garden. Raven started to clear the table. Kerstin helped him carry dishes into the kitchen, a large, well-scrubbed room filled with morning sunlight.

"I don't need your help," Raven said.

"Fine." Kerstin put down the cups she held just a trifle too sharply and marched out of the kitchen. She stood looking out the parlour window, but she didn't really see the harbour, nor the water beyond, dotted with fishing boats.

What should she do now? Join her father in the garden? He didn't seem eager for company. Wander around the town? Stay here with this prickly boy? Find Rilka and Gilles? But Gilles was as prickly as her son. And she didn't want their company. She wanted Alaric's. The view of the town and sea misted. Angrily, she blinked back tears.

"I'm sorry. I didn't mean to be rude. I just meant . . . You don't have to help."

Kerstin turned. Raven stood in the doorway, a slight flush staining his angular face.

"So you can be polite," Kerstin said waspishly, then was immediately ashamed. "I'm sorry," she said quickly. "But if you don't mind, I'd like to help. There's nothing else to do."

Raven nodded. Silently, they cleared the rest of the table and washed the dishes. Kerstin wondered whether the boy was always this quiet. She stole a sideways glance at him, and saw that he was frowning absently at the plate he'd been rubbing for at least the last two minutes.

"Raven," she said, "I won't say anything about meeting you on Atua, or about your bird. I promise."

Raven glanced at her and nodded before returning his attention to the plate.

Kerstin's lips tightened. He could say *something*, even if he couldn't bring himself to thank her. He was as hard to get along with as Gilles was.

Gilles. His mother. How did he feel, knowing his mother was in Morn but not with them? Would never be with them again? How would she feel if Star had left them to become a Wise Woman?

Star had not done that. She had left them to die.

And Alaric had left her to go to Uglessia, where he was falling in love with Redelle. And her father was leaving her, mentally if not physically, as he fell more and more in love with Rilka. There. She had said it, to herself at least.

A sob broke out before she could stop it.

Raven's head jerked around. "Is something wrong? I'm sorry. Did I do something? I didn't mean . . . Can I help? What is it?"

Kerstin shook her head vehemently. "No." She bit her lip, trying to regain control. How stupid to break down like this, in front of a strange boy, too. Another small sob escaped her. "Stupid . . . "

"No, it's not. Not if you feel like crying."

Surprised, she looked up to find him watching her with a worried frown. She shook her head again.

"I sometimes cry too," Raven said softly.

After a moment, Kerstin smiled at him. "Thank you." She sniffed and wiped her arm across her face.

He was kind. She had thought him prickly and rude. Prickly he might be, but in the middle of his own pain he could still be kind. What did she know about him, really know?

He had been on Atua, and wanted to keep his visit there a secret. He had a bird that always seemed to be watching her, a bird with which he had a strange affinity. He was the son of a woman who had great power with animals of all kinds.

Mirra had said her brother had no magic. Surely she would know. But . . .

"Raven, I know that men in Islandia are not supposed to possess any magical talent. But . . . Mirra said both sides of your family have strong gifts, and the way you seem to communicate with your raven . . . Do you have magic?"

Raven's face, so open and concerned a moment earlier, closed tighter than a clam shell. "Of course not," he said, returning to his washing. He cleaned each dish with short, angry swipes.

She shouldn't have spoken.

Yes, she should. If it were known that Raven had a gift, wouldn't that ease his family's pain? Mirra's guilt? She hesitated, not wanting another rebuff, then ploughed stubbornly on.

"You can communicate with your raven. I know you can."

Raven's hands stilled. He stood for a moment, then turned and faced her. "Men in Islandia do not have magic, at least not strong magic. It is impossible. As for the raven . . . I found it, abandoned, on the beach when it was a baby. I couldn't just leave it there. After all, I am its namesake." A small smile touched his lips. "I rescued it and raised it. I suppose I have inherited a bit of Mother's talent. I found I could communicate with it a little. I had to let it know that I was trying to help it, or it would have struggled and injured itself or me. The bond between us has deepened over the years."

Kerstin opened her mouth, but he stopped her. "But my raven is the only animal with which I can communicate at all clearly. Ask Mother if you don't believe me. She suspected too. I do not have a magical gift." So leave me alone, his eyes said. Begged.

Kerstin did. They finished the washing-up, then returned to the parlour where they stood uncertainly, not knowing what to do or say. They were rescued by a knock at the door.

It was Rilka.

"The Mother's blessings, Raven." She smiled at the boy, then turned to Kerstin. "I came to see if you want to accompany me as I visit the sick."

"Yes please." Kerstin jumped at the chance.

"Would your father — "

But Morgan was already there, answering the question for himself. "Freyn's Day, Rilka.

I'd be delighted to go with you to visit your patients."

Had he been watching for Rilka, hoping she would appear? Was that why he had stayed behind?

Suddenly, Kerstin wasn't at all eager to go out. All the same, she put on her cloak and left the house with them.

The early morning sunlight had clouded over. Rilka looked at the sky and shook her head.

"Rain before noon," she predicted.

They made their way through the town, stopping at houses where people needed Rilka's help: a small boy with a fever, a woman complaining of chronic headaches, a younger woman who was with child and having a hard time of it, an elderly man suffering from aching joints. At any other time, Kerstin would have been fascinated by Rilka's techniques, her use of herbs, her use of magic. But today she felt disgruntled, uncomfortable. Perhaps it was the way Rilka and Morgan talked and laughed together, the way their eyes met above a patient's bed. Kerstin felt unwanted and unneeded as she trailed after them through the busy streets.

By the time they emerged from the last house, light rain was spitting onto the dirt road. Rilka looked at the two Freyans doubtfully. "I want to see Delos, to make sure his arm is fully healed, but he lives up the beach a ways. Do you want to go back?"

Morgan shook his head. "A little rain never hurt us. At least — Kerstin, what do you want to do?"

"I think I'll go back to Mir's," Kerstin mumbled. The rain provided her with a welcome excuse to stop dragging behind them like a useless fifth wheel.

Morgan frowned. "All right." He turned to the Healer. "Rilka, I'm afraid we'll have to leave you here."

"I can go by myself!" Kerstin was outraged. Why was he treating her like a child? She had been independent for years.

"Not in a place where fights are breaking out between the townsfolk and Freyans. I can't have you go by yourself."

"I'll come with you then," Kerstin snapped.

"Are you sure?" Rilka looked worried. Did she think Kerstin would dissolve in the rain? Or maybe she just didn't want her with them. No. That was unfair. Rilka had invited her to come. It was she herself who wanted to be away from the two of them.

"Yes, I'm sure." What choice did she have?

They left the town and started walking up the beach towards a low stone hut that Kerstin could see in the distance. The beach was cluttered with rocks and branches, and Morgan took Rilka's arm several times to help her over them, though it didn't seem to Kerstin that his help was needed. She deliberately lagged behind the others. By the time they reached the hut, the rain was coming down steadily and she was thoroughly miserable.

Rilka knocked. After a minute, the door was inched open by a man Kerstin remembered from the healing huts. She instinctively looked at his arm, but it was covered by a long-sleeved shirt.

"What do you want?" His voice was gruff, forbidding.

"I thought, since I was on Moria, I could take a look at your arm and make sure you're fully recovered." Rilka smiled at him.

"I don't need your looking at it."

Rilka's smile faded. "I'm glad if it's healed, but I still should check it to make sure. Perhaps you don't recognise me," she added, as the man made no move to let them in. "I'm Rilka, the Healer."

"I know who you are."

They waited. The rain ran down Kerstin's neck and made rat's tails of her hair. She shivered.

Delos started to close the door.

Rilka held up a restraining hand. "Please, won't you let me take a look at your arm? Just to make sure it's healed? It will only take a minute."

"I said I don't need your help. I don't need the help of no Wise Woman."

"That's no way to speak to the woman who saved your life," Morgan said sharply. "All she wants to do is help you. You could at least be civil, if not grateful."

"Grateful. Huh! If the Wise Women didn't hog all the power to themselves, there'd of been someone here on the Island to help. I don't want no Wise Women." Delos glared at them all, then slammed the door in their faces. They were left standing in the rain.

"I don't understand." Hurt and confusion mingled in Rilka's voice.

"Don't worry about him. He's just an ungrateful, surly lout." Morgan looked as though he would like to kick the door — or, better still, the man behind it. Kerstin had rarely seen her father so angry.

"But I really should look at his arm. If it's not healing properly — "

"Don't worry about him," Morgan repeated more gently. "You can't force your help on him. Anyway, you did good work healing him. I'm sure he's fine."

"But — "

"Come. We should all get in out of the rain."

The walk back along the beach and through the now deserted streets was wet and silent. The talk and laughter that Kerstin had resented earlier was gone, but she couldn't even be thankful for that. She squelched and slogged her way along beside the others, keeping her head down to avoid the worst puddles. It seemed a long time before they arrived at Mir's door.

"I should return to the sisters' hut," Rilka said half-heartedly.

"You must get dry first, and wait for the rain to stop," Morgan said. Just then the door opened.

"You three look like drowned kittens," Ben said, ushering them in. Kerstin felt like one, as she shook some of the water off her cloak and bent to remove her muddy shoes. Mir, who was kneeling by the hearth lighting a fire, greeted them warmly and urged them to change quickly into dry clothes, then come and warm themselves by the fire.

"I have a spare dress you can borrow," Kerstin told Rilka. The Healer was slighter than she was, but much the same height. Rilka smiled gratefully and followed her upstairs.

They were soon changed and seated in front of the fireplace, sipping hot spiced drinks.

"Did you settle the fight?" Morgan asked.

"For now," Captain Merrigale said. "But I'm afraid bad feelings still run high — not surprisingly. Some of my men! . . . One even drew a knife and tried to use it. If it hadn't been for Ben, there'd have been blood shed today."

Kerstin looked at the wizard. "What happened?"

"As we were running towards the fight, I saw the flash of a knife in one of the sailor's hands. I think it was Swallowdale."

"It was," Captain Merrigale confirmed grimly. "He's one of the worst of the trouble-makers."

Ben continued. "I used a holding spell to prevent him from using the knife. I was worried the spell wouldn't work quickly enough to stop him, but it did."

"Thank Freyn," Captain Merrigale said. "Ben's action stopped the fight. By the time we reached the men, they were just standing there."

Mir smiled faintly. "The men of Morn were so amazed that a man could use magic that all they could do was stare. I was amazed too, even though Captain Merrigale had reported that you are learning the Wise Women's magic."

"I think we could learn from you, as well as you from us," Rilka said thoughtfully. "This holding spell sounds very useful."

There was a small silence, then Captain Merrigale sighed. "I just hope there are no more fights. I told my men that if there were, they'll be punished once we're on board ship. Bread and water only for the duration of the voyage." He sighed again. "But I've told them that before, and look what happened today."

"The fault was ours too," Mir said.

The captain grunted sceptically but didn't argue.

Kerstin sat quietly, listening to the talk and to the rain pounding on the roof. The flames flickered and leapt, creating dancing shadows on the faces around her. Mir was doing his best to be a genial host, but his face sagged into lines of unhappy worry when he wasn't talking. Rilka said little. She still looked confused and upset, and Morgan's eyes, when they drifted her way, which they did frequently, were concerned.

"You're very quiet, Rilka," Ben said. "Is something wrong?"

She shook her head. "It's just . . . I don't understand. Delos sounded so angry."

"What's this?" Mir asked.

Morgan explained since Rilka seemed reluctant to do so. Mir shook his head at the end of the tale. "Delos is notoriously gruff. He hates to admit to any weakness and guards his privacy jealously. I wouldn't worry about his words — or his arm. He's been back fishing for weeks."

"But he sounded so angry, not just at me but at all the Wise Women."

"He isn't the only one who's angry at the Wise Women." Raven's voice came unexpectedly from the shadowy corner where he was sitting. Kerstin started. He'd been so still she'd scarcely been aware of his presence.

"What's that?" Mir asked sharply, turning to stare at him. They all did.

Raven shifted uncomfortably and looked down at his hands.

"What do you mean?" Mir asked.

"I . . . Some of the men have been talking. They don't like it that the Wise Women have all the power. They think it should be shared."

"But it can't be," Rilka protested.

Raven looked at her, then away. "They say the Wise Women should live here and on the other islands, where their help is needed, not on Atua."

"Who is 'they'?" Mir demanded.

Raven shrugged. "Some of the men in town, especially those who've become friends with the Freyans. The sailors say it's wrong that women hold all the power."

Swain Netter and his friends, Kerstin thought.

"How do you know all this?" Mir asked, his eyes fixed on his son's face.

Raven's gaze shifted. "I've overheard some talk," he mumbled. He hesitated, then looked straight at his father. "A couple of men have talked to me, too, thinking I might agree with them."

"And do you?"

Raven paused before answering. "I . . . don't know." He and Mir stared at each other. Rilka made a small sound and stretched out her hand as though in protest, then dropped it. Kerstin looked from Raven to Mir, then away. The silence was heavy. It went on and on.

Mir broke it finally. "We will talk of this later, without burdening our guests. Rilka, I am sorry. I hope you know how much everyone in Morn — or almost everyone, it would appear — values you."

"Thank you," Rilka murmured. She smiled, but her smile was troubled. "I really must go. The rain is tapering off." So it was. The pounding on the roof had thinned to a light patter.

Morgan rose. "I'll go with you."

They left. A moment later, Kerstin escaped to her room, pleading a headache.

THE CIRCLE

LOVE

The woman on the bed was in pain. Kerstin could feel, almost as though in her own bones, the aching, crippling hurt in the old arthritic body. If only she could reach deeper, not only soothe the pain but cure the illness. She had learned, now, how to ease a pinched nerve, how to move along the paths that fed headaches and stop them, how to staunch a wound. But this . . . She frowned, feeling the woman's disappointment and her own.

"Enough," a voice said softly in her ear — or was it her mind? Kerstin shook her head irritably.

"Enough," the voice repeated. A hand was placed on her shoulder. At the same time, a mind nudged her gently but firmly away from the woman's body, the woman's suffering. Kerstin blinked the world back into focus and saw Rilka smiling down at her.

"You are doing very well," the Healer said. "But this is too much for you. Let me."

Reluctantly, Kerstin stood up and moved away from the cot in the healing hut, allowing Rilka to kneel in her place. The Healer smiled warmly at her patient and put her hands over the crippled, rheumatic ones.

"Relax, Ceri. In a short time, the pain will go."

The old woman smiled back trustingly and closed her eyes. Kerstin watched as Rilka bent her head, a frown of concentration lining her face. The only sounds in the hut were the deep breaths of the Healer and her patient, breathing in identical rhythm. Kerstin almost forgot to breathe herself as she stood, motionless. There was no great surge of power, but it seemed to her that a gentle breeze sprang up, bringing with it the sweet scent of honeysuckle. The lines of pain eased from Ceri's face, and a smile touched her sleeping lips. Rilka rose stiffly and motioned Kerstin outside.

The girl squinted against the hot glare of the sun as they emerged. Bees hummed and crickets chirped in the grass.

"She will rest now, and wake with no pain," Rilka said softly.

"Why couldn't I help her?" Kerstin demanded.

"Rheumatic pain goes deep. It is hard to heal, as I know to my sorrow. I have had my failures." Rilka was silent a minute, head bent, then returned her attention to Kerstin. "Do not worry. You have learned very quickly and show great talent, more so than either Ben or your father, though they too have learned a great deal."

Kerstin flushed, pleased with the praise. But then, she should be doing well. She had thrown herself fiercely into the work ever since their return from Moria three months ago. All the same . . .

"Will I ever be able to help people like Ceri?"

Rilka hesitated. "I don't know," she said finally. "You have great gifts for magic, but . . . "

"But?"

"But you are not an Islandian Healer."

"And only Islandians can become healers? Is that what you mean?" Kerstin's flush had deepened into anger.

"I don't know, Kerstin. I only know what is true in Islandia. Here, only one person in each generation is born with the true gift, the gift of the best, deepest healing. It may be different for Freyans. Perhaps, in time, you will be able to do all that a true Healer can do."

"But you don't think so."

Rilka's hesitation was longer this time. Then she shook her head. "No."

Kerstin's hands clenched into fists. She wanted to argue. She wanted to lash out. But Rilka's kind brown eyes, watching her with concerned sincerity, defeated her as always. Silently, she turned away.

"Kerstin — "

"I think I'll go do some weeding in the herb garden. If you don't mind."

"No, of course not."

Kerstin trudged up the path, feeling as leaden as the sultry, heavy air. It was unusually hot for Atua, with no trace of the cool sea breeze that ordinarily freshened the air. A fly landed on her hair. Irritated, she brushed it away.

Morgan was alone in the garden, weeding industriously. Too bad he doesn't work this hard in our garden at home, Kerstin thought sourly. But then I don't either, she reminded herself. She bit her lip, picturing her mother's disappointed face if she could see her beloved garden today.

"Where's Master Grantwish?" she asked as she joined her father.

"He's with Jaine. She's showing him something of Islandian weather magic. A good day for it." Morgan cast his own weather-wise eyes upwards. "The air's broody, ready to storm."

Kerstin nodded silently and began to pull up weeds.

"Where's Rilka?" Morgan's voice was just a bit too casual. Kerstin glanced at him sharply.

"Still at the healing huts." She paused, then burst out, "She said I'd never be a true Healer."

Morgan looked surprised. "But you're doing so well. I'm sure she's pleased with your progress."

"Maybe. But she still doesn't think I'll ever be a true Healer. Not like she is."

Morgan sat back on his heels and regarded her thoughtfully. "No," he agreed. "None of us will probably ever be Healers like Rilka. I've given up hope for that. We've learned so much, though, all of us, and by the time we return to Freya we'll know even more. I can be content with that."

By the time they returned to Freya, six weeks from now, it would be too late to go to Uglessia. To Alaric. And she wouldn't even return a true Healer.

As though reading her thoughts, Morgan said, "I wonder how Alaric is."

"I have no idea," Kerstin said shortly.

Morgan looked at her strangely, but said nothing and asked no questions. They worked silently while the sun beat down on them.

Wings beat above her. Kerstin looked up. With no surprise, she saw the familiar sheen of black feathers as the raven settled onto the branch of a tree. Raven's raven. She grimaced, but in truth she didn't really resent the bird's hovering presence as much as before their visit to Moria.

How was Raven? Following his comments about the Wise Women, he had been under a cloud of disapproval. Mir had tried to hide his anger from the Freyans, but he watched his son as though Raven were some unpredictable wild creature, and spoke to him in short, brusque commands when he spoke at all. Raven had been more silent and withdrawn than ever. And Mirra, obviously wishing she hadn't spoken so frankly, had said very little to Kerstin for the rest of their stay in Morn. Kerstin had been glad to leave. Not that their return trip had been pleasant. Rilka was still upset by her encounter with Delos, and Morgan was troubled by her mood. As for Gilles! . . . Knowing her history, Kerstin had tried to feel sympathetic, but the woman's sharp-edged comments and brittle silences made it difficult. Only Ben had tried to maintain pleasant conversation, and even he had faltered after a while. Kerstin had scrambled out of the boat onto Atua's marshy western shore with a sigh of relief.

What would the raven show her if she could see through its eyes? What would it show her of Raven? Of his family? Of Morn, with its conflicts between Morians and Freyans?

"Have you heard any news from Morn?" she asked.

Morgan looked up, frowning. "More trouble, I'm afraid. The man who came to the healing huts last week with a knife wound received it in a fight with one of Merrigale's men."

"I didn't know that," she said, shocked.

He nodded grimly. "Rilka was talking to the fellow about the situation there. The fighting is bad. Even worse, though, is that some of the men have become friends with the sailors, and side with them against their fellow townsfolk. The feeling's bad."

"Oh no." She thought of Mir's worried face. "Maybe we should leave soon, before there's more trouble." Then she heard her own words and caught her breath. Why not leave soon? Very soon? She would be glad to go. And the earlier they left, the better her chances of crossing the mountains before the snows fell, of joining Alaric.

"We should leave *now*," she said loudly.

Morgan shook his head.

"Why not? The ship must be repaired by now. I know Captain Merrigale doesn't want to leave only to have to sail back in a month or six weeks, no matter how much trouble his sailors cause. But he doesn't have to. We can go with him. If we leave now, we can remove the sailors before they do more harm."

"No. We haven't learned all we came to learn."

"You said yourself that we've learned a lot."

"But not everything."

"When will we know everything? We could stay twenty years and still not know everything, especially since we'll never be true Healers." Kerstin was on her feet, trembling with the force of her argument.

"I want to learn more before we leave."

"But — "

"We're not leaving right now, Kerstin," Morgan said quietly. Definitely. He returned to his weeding.

"But it doesn't make sense — "

"I don't want to hear any more."

Kerstin stared at her father. He'd *never* done this to her before. He'd always been willing to listen to her arguments, to discuss things with her. But not now.

"It's because of Rilka, isn't it?" she blurted out.

Morgan looked up sharply. "What's that?"

"It's because of Rilka, isn't it?" she persisted. "You're in love with her and don't want to leave her."

He became very still. In the silence, Kerstin's words echoed loudly.

Morgan looked down at his hands. He dusted them off. Then he looked up again at his daughter. His face was suddenly tired.

"I suppose I am," he said quietly. "I've never said so in those words to myself, but I suppose I am." He fell silent.

Kerstin wished she hadn't spoken.

He said nothing more for some time. When he spoke again, his voice was gentle. "Do you mind? Loving Rilka doesn't mean that I love Star less, you know."

"I . . . I don't . . . ," Kerstin stammered. She wasn't ready for this. She didn't know what to say. She did mind. Didn't she? At last she managed, "She's not much like Mother."

"I suppose not. In some ways they're alike, and in some ways . . . no. There can only be one Star. And one Rilka," he added softly. Kerstin ached at the tenderness in his voice.

"I guess it doesn't really make much difference how I feel," she said, trying to sound mature and matter-of-fact.

"No." He stood suddenly, his voice hard, flat. "It doesn't make much difference how you feel, or how I feel, or how Rilka feels. I have no idea whether she returns my love or not, but it doesn't make any difference. She is a sister, and can neither marry nor leave the Circle. So I shall return to Freya the way I came — alone. As for when we return . . . maybe you're right. Maybe I'm delaying our departure because I want to be near Rilka as long as possible. I don't think so, but maybe I'm wrong. I'll think about it." He turned and left the garden.

Kerstin watched him go, swallowing hard. She wanted to run after him and hug him, but didn't. What did he mean, he was returning to Freya the way he had come — alone? Did she count for nothing?

With a raucous cry, the raven rose from the tree and flew off. Kerstin kicked the ground viciously.

"Laugh! Go ahead, laugh! I'd laugh too if I could. Love! I hate it!"

Incoming Tide

Kerstin ran. Away from the garden, the Circle, the sisters. Away from them all. Panting, sweating, she ran. She slowed when she approached the healing huts. Swerving, she entered the cover of the trees.

It was only as she scrambled up the steep slope at the far end of the valley that she realised where she was heading. Towards the eastern shore. Towards the sea that separated her from Freya.

Then she was at the top. Below her lay the ocean, its waves rolling and breaking into white foam on the jagged rocks and pebbly beach. Why, oh why wasn't she on a ship right now? A ship going home.

She started to run down the hill towards the beckoning sea. Loose stones rolled out from beneath her feet. She teetered. Almost fell.

Then she managed to right herself, and made her way more cautiously.

The tide was out. She walked across the wet, rocky beach towards the line of breakers.

Stooping, she picked up a round stone, worn smooth by the sea, and hurled it at the foam. For a long time she stood, watching the waves. Then she turned and walked slowly along the shore, head down, kicking loose stones as she went.

Time passed. She walked and walked. Finally, tired muscles forced her to stop. She sat down on a large, flat rock and looked out to sea.

The sea had vanished. So had the hills behind her, hidden by dense white fog. Even as she watched, tendrils of mist drew closer to her. Thickened.

Alarmed, Kerstin slid off the rock. She must get back. But how far had she come? How could she find the path over the hills? Maybe she should stay where she was. But no. The fog might last for hours, even days. Her father, Rilka, everyone would be worried. They'd send out a search party, the way they would for a lost child. No.

Slowly, cautiously, she started walking back up the beach, hands groping in front of her. The fog touched her skin with cool, damp fingers.

She could hear her footsteps, her panting breath, the pounding of the surf. But the fog muffled sounds, making everything seem far away.

Water surged around her feet. Kerstin gasped. Of course! The tide was coming in. She started to move back. Too late. A large wave caught her, tugged her off her feet.

Water filled her mouth, her nose. She struggled for breath, for air, for solid footing. Then her head broke free of the wave. She fell to her knees, scraping them badly, scratching her hands as she scrabbled for purchase, tried to stand. The undertow caught her and pulled.

She couldn't breathe. She couldn't see. She couldn't stand. She was lost. Lost and drowning.

Another wave took her and tossed her towards shore. She gasped and spat water as her head emerged again. Pain gashed her hand as she grabbed the sharp stones of the seabed, dragging herself forward. She staggered to her feet just as the insidious undertow tugged her back. She fell.

This time she was ready, knowing another wave would come. When it did, she rode with it and threw herself forward as it receded, flinging out her hands to grasp solid ground.

Her right hand came down on something small and round and spiny. Pain. Searing. Lancing.

Kerstin's scream pierced the fog and waves, shocking her as much as her pain did. For a moment she stayed motionless, too shocked to move, staring at her hand. There was no blood. What? . . .

Then she knew.

She had put her hand on a spinella. And spinellas were poisonous.

What had Mirra said about them? She couldn't remember. It didn't matter now anyway. She could feel the water tugging, gathering momentum. Sobbing hoarsely, she dug her left hand into the wet ground and hauled herself forward. Rocks scraped her face and body, but she didn't even notice the small hurts as pain from her right hand tore through her.

Just a little further. A little further and she could rest.

She collapsed in the lee of a large boulder, lying on her back with her right arm draped limply across her chest. Ragged, sobbing breaths shuddered through her.

The world faded in and out with every jab of pain.

The pain was spreading. The poison was spreading. She must do something. Make a tourniquet. Would that help? Would anything help?

With a great effort, Kerstin dragged herself up till she was half sitting, half reclining against the rock. She managed to tug her petticoat off. Holding it between her teeth, she tried to pull off a strip with her one good hand. A small slit appeared, but nothing more. The cloth was too strong and too wet. Sobbing in frustration, she tried again. And again. There! She had a strip.

But tying it tight, fumbling with her left hand and her teeth, stopping while the fog swirled around her and the world shifted in and out . . . She couldn't do it. She looked at the rag bound around her arm and knew it would do no good. A line of red was spreading up the vein in her arm. With a shuddering sob, she sank back to the ground.

Only a Healer could help. That's what Mirra had said.

She needed Rilka.

But Rilka was across the hills, oblivious.

She could mind-call.

She couldn't clear her mind. She couldn't concentrate. Her image of Rilka, of herself lying on the beach, kept wavering, disappearing into the mist. Into the pain.

Perhaps if she sat up . . . She gritted her teeth and pushed herself halfway up. Swayed. Fell into a black hole that wanted to swallow her.

No! She mustn't lose consciousness. She must try again.

She tried. Rested. Tried.

Her calls were so feeble, so confused. Only someone very close would hear them.

Maybe the sisters at the Circle would miss her, realise something was wrong. Her father could use a finding spell. But they wouldn't know she was gone till dinnertime. And dinnertime came late on summer evenings.

Even then, it would take time before they became really worried.

What time was it? She had no idea. Time was measured by the ache in her arm, which surged and ebbed, surged and ebbed. Like the tides of the sea. The sea that had tried to drown her.

Had she survived the sea only to die here?

She was a Healer. Well, almost a Healer. Healer, heal yourself.

Rilka said that was the hardest thing to do, to heal yourself.

She must try.

She tried to concentrate on the veins in her body. The veins, where venom ran, swift and deadly.

She couldn't focus. Her mind kept drifting into mist, like the mist that surrounded her.

She must.

The effort was too much. The world tilted. Swam. She fell into darkness.

When she opened her eyes again, the mist around her seemed to have thinned, but maybe that was only because the mist in her head had thickened. She thought she saw two bright black eyes above her. Was it possible? . . . She stirred feebly.

"Help!" she called, her voice a faint, raspy croak. There was no answer. Were the eyes only in her imagination? She closed her own eyes. When she looked again, she saw only mist.

She was so cold. If only the sun would come out and dry her sodden clothes. She couldn't stop shivering. The pain seemed less, but she was so weak. Too weak to use her mind, her magic. All these years studying, learning, striving to be a wizard — the youngest, most powerful wizard in Freya. That had been her dream. There had been other dreams. To help Yrwith and Uglessia. Well, at least she had done that. To heal. To marry Alaric and live with him in the old house on Wizard's Hill. Her newest dream. Were they all to die here on this rocky beach?

No! With one last, fierce effort she mind-called. "Help! Help! Help!" till her strength failed and she slipped back into darkness.

There were colours in the darkness, grey swirling clouds stabbed by flashing slashes of red. A yellow dot shone dimly in the distance. The sun? She had wanted the sun. Gradually the yellow grew, became brighter and closer. Warmed her. There was green too, or was it blue? A cool, restful blue. She was being rocked to sleep on a calm, cradling sea under the light of a healing sun, with someone's hand holding her safe.

She smiled, and slept.

The sun had set and the first faint stars of night were pale candles in the dusky blue sky. Kerstin lay watching them for a time. Then she sat up abruptly.

There was no pain. She was stiff and sore from lying on the beach, but the terrible pain had gone. She stared at her arm in the dim light. Her flesh was clean. There were no lines of angry red.

Mirra had said people always died of spinella poison unless a Healer . . .

Had she healed herself? She couldn't believe it. She had spent her last strength in a desperate cry for help. Rilka, then? But Rilka wasn't here. No one was.

But someone was coming. More than one person. A line of moving lanterns was heading up the beach, straight towards her. She grimaced. A search party, undoubtedly. Now that she was well and the fog was gone, she wished it hadn't come. Slowly, she rose and went to meet it.

"Kerstin!" Morgan ran the last few yards and seized her in a fierce hug. "Are you all right?"

"I'm fine."

He held her away from him and searched her face. "You're sure? We were so worried. I thought . . . I tried a finding spell, you see, when the sisters came to me. That wasn't until after supper. They thought you were with Rilka in the healing huts. At first I couldn't find you. Even when I did, the impression was so faint — "

"I was asleep."

"Asleep?"

She cleared her throat. "I was caught by the fog and tide, and landed in the ocean. After I struggled to shore, I . . . I stayed for a while. The fog . . . I waited for it to lift. Then I guess

I must have fallen asleep. I'm sorry. I didn't mean to worry you."

Morgan shook his head. "As long as you're all right. That's all that matters."

"It was my fault." Ben sounded more miserable than she had ever heard him. "Jaine was showing me Islandian weather magic. She wanted to bring in cool moist air before a violent storm could break. I asked to do it, but I'm still not used to air patterns here. The fog moved in too quickly. I didn't even obey the first law of wizardry, to check to make sure no one would be hurt by my actions."

"I didn't check either, and I was your teacher," Jaine said quietly. "I'm sorry, Kerstin."

"It's all right. I'm fine." Kerstin smiled at the stocky sister, at all of them. Rilka, Teira and Alannis had come as well as Jaine and the two wizards. And Gilles was there too, she noted with surprise.

Alannis spoke in her most practical voice. "Now that we've found her, shall we return as quickly as possible so Kerstin can get out of her wet clothes and we can all retire for the night?"

Morgan placed a protective arm around Kerstin's shoulders as they headed back down the beach towards the darkening hills. She took one last look backwards as they left, and shivered.

Why had she said nothing about the spinella? Because the memory was so confused in her mind? Because she couldn't even explain to herself, much less to anyone else, what had happened? Or because she was sure a hand had held hers as she lay unconscious and dying on the beach? She hadn't died. Why?

THROUGH RAVEN'S EYES

Kerstin found it hard to sleep that night. Questions kept tugging at her mind, and pictures wouldn't leave her alone. Pictures of herself struggling in the sea, putting her hand on a small, spiny body, lying on the beach. When she finally fell into fitful sleep, it was coloured by wild, disturbing dreams.

In the days that followed, Kerstin watched her father anxiously. He reminded her of a candle that was burning low. Even his passion to learn more about healing seemed quenched. Ben, sensitive to his friend's mood, was less cheerful than usual, and sometimes looked at Morgan with a worried frown.

If only they could leave Islandia now. But Morgan refused to go, and there was nothing Kerstin could say that would change his mind.

Had he spoken of his love to Rilka? The Healer, while as courteous and helpful as ever, had dark circles under her eyes and was easily startled. She and Morgan rarely looked at each other now.

They had fewer opportunities to do so, for Amary had decided that the Freyans should spend some time becoming familiar with the other magical gifts. Kerstin was glad. The new challenges distracted her, and the knowledge she gained was fascinating.

She was less than happy, however, when she was told she was to work with Gilles.

The day after Kerstin's encounter with the spinella, Gilles had left to visit the island of Lotos. Kerstin had hoped, vainly, that she would stay away until it was time for them to depart. But to her surprise, she found her time with the woman interesting, even enjoyable. True, Gilles did not welcome her with open arms. But she was civil, and did her best to be patient.

Gilles was different when she was with animals. Absorbed in her work, her face relaxed. The lines of strain and bitterness eased. This is the way she should always be, Kerstin thought, watching with wonder as Gilles effortlessly moved the sheep the way she wanted and retrieved honey from the beehive without a worry. Kerstin, accompanying her to the hive, was fully encased in protective clothing. It was with the sick and damaged animals, though, that the Animal Helper truly demonstrated her skill.

On Kerstin's fourth day with her, Gilles suddenly raised her head from her milking. She seemed to listen for a minute, then rose. "A vixen has fallen and hurt herself. I must go to her."

Kerstin looked up eagerly from her own milking. "May I come?"

"No. You'd frighten her," Gilles said brusquely.

Kerstin bit her lip.

"Anyway, the cows need you to finish the milking," Gilles added, a bit more gently, before striding off.

Two hours later she was back with an injured fox lying quietly in her arms. She laid it carefully on a bed of straw in the shed where she kept sick and injured wildlife — a sparrow with a broken wing, a chipmunk that lay list-lessly, viewing the world through dulled eyes. Gilles examined the vixen's leg with swift, sure fingers. The animal winced once or twice but lay quietly, gazing at her with trust.

"What do you see?" Gilles asked suddenly.

Kerstin looked at her in surprise. "See?"

"Through her eyes. In her mind."

Kerstin blinked. Yesterday Gilles had guided her into the minds of a sheep and a cow, and she had received vague, dim impressions of grass and sun and the smells of other animals. But could she make the journey on her own? She stilled her mind and used all the skills she had learned from Alannis and Rilka. Nothing happened.

"She's a fox, not a person," Gilles said sharply.

"I know that." Kerstin's voice was equally sharp.

Gilles looked up with a sudden, unexpected smile. "Sorry. I'm not the best teacher in the world. Think of trees and forest paths and the smells and sounds you'd find in the woods. Then try seeing."

Kerstin did. After a few minutes images — blurred, a bit distorted, but images — came to her mind. Padding four-footed over mossy ground. Catching a scent, a scent that promised food for herself and her cubs. Running. Falling. Pain, sharp, tearing. Fear. And now, lying on the straw, there was still pain, still fear, but they were dulled, soothed, under the caring, protective hands.

"Good," Gilles said. "Now let her know that she has nothing to fear from you, that you want to help her."

Cautiously, Kerstin projected a reassuring message.

"Not that way. She doesn't think in words. Show her."

For a moment, Kerstin hesitated, perplexed. Then she looked at the fox again, at its red sides moving up and down in quiet breaths, at its slender legs, one of them askew in Gilles' hand. She sent a picture of her hands touching the leg, of the vixen rising on it, running free.

"That's better. Hold her leg so I can bind it. She'll let you, now."

She did. Kerstin felt a thrill of pride and pleasure as she held the furred leg and watched Gilles splint it.

"There. Rest now and have no fear. I will take food to your cubs until you are well enough," Gilles murmured. Kerstin caught a vision of the woman approaching a hidden cave, of four small bodies tumbling over each other in their eagerness to reach the food she brought.

As they left the shed, Gilles turned to Kerstin. "You did well. Much better than I expected."

A small warm glow spread through Kerstin at these words, the first signs of praise Gilles had given her. It was because of them that she dared ask about Raven later that day, as they were walking towards the sheep pasture.

The raven was sitting on a poplar branch in a small copse of trees near the pasture. Kerstin stopped and eyed it thoughtfully. She hadn't seen the bird lately. In fact, she hadn't seen it since the day she'd spoken to her father in the herb garden. Or had she seen it later? Later the same day, when she'd thought bright sharp eyes were peering at her through the fog.

"Gilles," she said hesitantly, "I know it's thought in Islandia that men don't have magical powers, but is it possible? . . . Raven . . . It sometimes seems to me — "

"No." Gilles had gone still at the mention of her son. Kerstin looked at her closed face and almost gave up. But there was the bird. And the beach, and the watching eyes in the fog. None of the Wise Women had healed her. She did not believe she had healed herself. Then who?

"I know the gifts run in families, and that both you and Mir — "

"No." After a moment, the woman added grudgingly, "I suppose it's the raven that makes you wonder." Her eyes flickered to the raven, then away again. "Yes, my son has talent with animals, but it is a small talent, less than yours, I think. The only animal with which he communicates really well is this bird, and that is because of the bond between them. He saved it when it was a baby, and has raised it ever since."

"Yes, I know."

"Then why these questions? Why bring the subject up?"

Kerstin flushed at the anger she heard in the woman's voice. She glanced at the raven once more. Were her suspicions ridiculous? Had she merely dreamed those eyes, seen through the fog on the beach, the fog in her mind? If they had been there, was it only coincidence? Or had she dreamed the entire incident? The eyes watched her, beady, bright, familiar. Very familiar. She took a deep breath.

"If Raven hasn't inherited your gift, could he have inherited his father's?"

"His father's?" Gilles' voice and eyebrows shot up.

"I know Mir isn't a Healer, but he is related to Rilka. The gift for healing runs in his family."

"The Mother's gifts do not descend through the male line," Gilles said shortly.

"But — "

"Enough! Enough of this foolish talk! We have work to do. *If* you'd care to help, that is." Gilles stalked away.

Kerstin glared after her, then returned her attention to the raven. *Was* she being foolish? Maybe. But suddenly, desperately, she wanted to talk to Raven.

Could she use her new ability to arrange a meeting? The idea made her catch her breath.

Clenching her teeth in concentration, she tried to see through the bird's eyes. Gradually, a picture formed in her mind. Green grass. On the grass, a creature with brown on top, blue beneath, and a whitish blob in between. Herself, she realised with a start. Herself, seen from above. Seen through raven's eyes. She hurled pictures at the bird's mind, the same pictures over and over again. Raven, sailing through the dusk of evening over the narrow channel that divided the two islands. Raven meeting her on the western shore.

With a harsh croak, the raven rose from its perch and flew off to the west. Kerstin watched it go, wondering. Had the bird received her pictures? Would it show them to Raven? Would Raven understand?

She turned and walked after Gilles.

The light was dim by the time Kerstin descended the last hill onto the marshy beach. Summer was not yet over, but already the days were getting shorter. It won't be too much longer before we can go home, Kerstin promised herself.

Pleading fatigue, she had gone to her room immediately after supper. There, she had glanced dubiously at the small window, then decided on an old, familiar spell instead. Invisible to all but a hard, direct stare, she had walked back through the hall and out the door. She would return the same way. She wasn't an apprentice wizard for nothing.

There was no sign of bird or boy. Was she crazy, thinking Raven would receive her message, that he would come? It would be late by the time she got back. How long should she wait?

If Raven did come, did answer her call, what should she say to him?

Then she saw the white sail and slender bow of a small boat. It was close to shore and drawing yet nearer. She would have noticed it earlier if there had been more light. She watched it land, then walked slowly down to the water's edge to meet its occupant.

"What do you want?" Raven demanded as soon as he had waded ashore and beached the boat. The raven rode his shoulder.

"You came."

He said nothing.

"I wasn't sure my message was clear."

"It was clear enough. You've learned a lot. What do you want?" he repeated.

"To talk."

"About what?"

She hesitated. "Look, can't we sit down somewhere?"

"Is this going to take long? I don't want to be too late getting home."

"Will you be safe sailing home in the dark?" she asked, alarmed. She hadn't thought of possible danger for him when she'd sent her call.

"I'll be fine," he said impatiently. "But Father won't be pleased if I return home at midnight."

"Oh. Well, I won't be long. I just wanted to ask you something."

"Then ask."

She gave up any idea of being subtle. "Did you heal me?" she demanded.

There was a brief pause. "Heal you?" he repeated. "Heal you of what? Why would you think I healed you? How could I heal you? I'm no Wise Woman." He laughed scornfully.

His answer was definite. But there was something in his voice . . .

"But you are a healer."

"Don't be silly. Rilka is the Healer. Anyway, boys can't be Healers. Or anything else," he added. Was there a touch of bitterness in his voice?

"You are," she insisted stubbornly. "I was poisoned by a spinella and you came and saved me."

He was silent for a moment. Then he asked, "Why do you think it was I who healed you? Anyway, how would I know that you needed help, or get to — wherever it was you were?" he added.

"I don't know how you got there," she said slowly, thinking it out. "Maybe you were close by in your boat, or on Atua already. You seem to spend a lot of time here. But you knew I needed help because your bird saw me."

His hand lifted instinctively to stroke the raven's feathers. She wished she could see his eyes, but the light was too dim.

"It's true, isn't it? Deny it if you can."

This time the silence dragged on and on. He turned and looked out at the darkening sea. She reached out a restraining hand, afraid he would go.

He sighed and turned back to her. "Look, Kerstin, even if it were true — and I'm not saying it is — but even if it were, it wouldn't mean anything."

She stared at him. "Not mean anything? Raven, it means that you've inherited the gift of healing, that you're a true Healer."

"No!" His denial rang with pain.

She gaped at him. "Why do you say that? You must know what you can do. What you are."

"No." He shook his head stubbornly.

"But . . . I know it's thought in Islandia that only women have magic. But that's just not true. You do have magic."

"If I did, what would that make me?"

"But . . . In Freya — " Kerstin stopped. In Freya, most wizards were men. But not all. How would she feel if she were the only female wizard in Freya? More than that. How would she feel if she'd been told all her life that she could never be a wizard? That it was biologically impossible for her to have any magical talent — the talent she knew she did have?

"Yes, I know. In Freya men have magic. That's why I was so curious when you and your father and his friend came here. But it doesn't matter. We're not in Freya. I'm not a Freyan."

"But it must be terrible, having such a gift and not being able to use it. If you told people, if you showed them — "

"No. Even if it were true, what would happen if I told people, showed them, as you suggest? Can you imagine the Wise Women letting me or any man into the Circle?"

She was silent.

"You see? I would only be thought strange, more strange than I already am."

"Tell your family, at least. Surely — "

"No. What good would that do, knowing they have an unnatural son? They don't need that pain too. No. I would never tell anyone I had magic. If I did have it, that is," he added carefully. "And you must promise to say nothing too."

She frowned.

"Please," he said quietly. A small breeze stirred his hair and ruffled the raven's feathers.

"I'll promise if you insist," Kerstin said slowly. "Raven, I owe you my life. I wouldn't do anything to hurt you. But I can't believe this is right. You have such a marvellous gift. It's such a waste not to use it."

"Promise."

"All right. I promise," she said reluctantly.

He gave a sigh of relief. "Thank you." He looked out to sea again. "I must go."

"Yes. Thank you for coming."

He bent and began to push the boat towards the water. It was almost completely dark. The waves lapped quietly against the shore.

A thought struck Kerstin. "What will you do if someone else needs your help? In public?"

He paused, then shook his head and climbed into his boat without a word.

Kerstin watched him until the boat was only a dark speck on the darker sea. Then she turned to start her long walk back. She was glad she had brought a lantern. The moon was hidden by clouds, and the world seemed very black.

GILLES

During the next two days, Gilles limited her talk with Kerstin to terse commands as they went about their daily chores and tended the sick and injured animals. Kerstin made a few attempts at friendly conversation, but these were ignored. The girl leashed her fraying temper with difficulty. She had to talk to Gilles about Raven. Oh, not directly. She had made a promise, after all. But surely there must be some indirect way to make the woman see.

Talking to Gilles wasn't easy, however. But then, on her last day with the Animal Helper, Kerstin looked over and saw a faint smile on Gilles' face. They were sitting in the barn, milking. Gilles' hands moved in smooth, rhythmic motions. Beyond the open door, a gentle rain fell.

"It seems odd," Kerstin said, trying to make her tone casual, as though she were musing out loud about something abstract, unimportant, "that in Freya I was one of very few female wizards, while here it's thought that only women have magical power."

Gilles said nothing. Kerstin waited a moment, then asked, still casually, "Has there ever been a man with magic here?"

Gilles threw her a suspicious glance, then returned her attention to the cow she was milking. "No."

"Never? Perhaps there were men who had power but were told they couldn't use it."

"If there have been, I've never heard of them," Gilles said shortly.

This was less than encouraging. For a moment, Kerstin's hands stopped moving on the warm, soft udder. The cow made a low noise of protest, and she quickly resumed milking. She said, her eyes firmly fixed on the cow's brown flank, "I wonder . . . If it were ever thought possible that men possessed magic, do you think some would come forward and say they did?"

"What do you mean?" Gilles stopped milking and swung around to face Kerstin, black eyes narrowed.

Kerstin floundered. "Well . . . I just meant, if men think it's impossible for them to have magic, maybe they hide it, even from themselves. Maybe — "

"Maybe you should stop interfering in what doesn't concern you."

Kerstin felt as though she'd been slapped. She stopped milking again and stared at Gilles as the woman continued with barely suppressed fury. "You come here as an outsider and ask for our help. We give it to you. We have even taken you within the Circle. You know nothing about us, but you try to change us, to make us more like yourself."

Kerstin was white. "It's just . . . just that I know how frustrating it would be, how . . . how empty I would feel, if I weren't allowed to practise magic at home because I'm a girl."

"And that gives you the right to upset things here in Islandia? In my family? Oh, yes, I know that you think my son has power. You refuse to believe it's impossible. That's what this is all about, isn't it?"

Kerstin went from white to red. "You won't even look at the possibility that Raven has power. Despite the fact that magic runs so strongly in your family on both sides. Despite Solande's dreams." For a moment she faltered, despite her anger. She was coming dangerously close to breaking her promise. Then she continued, stubbornly. "That's not fair."

Gilles' hands clenched, but she spoke with forced calm. "If anyone in my family were to inherit magic, it would be my daughter, not my son."

"But Mirra hasn't."

Gilles' shoulders slumped. "No. Mirra hasn't," she agreed tonelessly, and turned back to the cow.

Watching her, Kerstin felt her anger ebbing away. Perhaps she should say no more. But it's *not* fair, she reminded herself. It's not fair that Mirra feels guilty. It's not fair that Raven has to hide his gift.

"So why did Solande dream as she did?" she demanded. As soon as the words were out, she wished them back.

Gilles' hands stopped milking. She sat very still for a moment, then turned and faced the girl.

"Who knows why Solande dreams as she does? Who knows why she dreamed that I should marry Mir, and later that I should leave my family and join the Circle? I would have been happy enough as a girl to know my future lay here. Not that I didn't love Mir, but I felt such a calling . . . But that was not what Solande dreamed. Not then. So I married and had children, and we grew together in love, Mir and I and our children. But then the former Animal Helper died, suddenly, unexpectedly, and Solande dreamed again."

She fell silent. Kerstin looked down, abashed by the storm of unhappiness she had unleashed.

"I'm sorry," she murmured.

Gilles rose suddenly, with a jerky movement that upset the milk bucket and sent it spinning and clattering on the floor.

"Sorry. Oh, yes, you're sorry. And Solande is sorry. And much good that does me or Mir. And Solande, with her dreams, will never dream that Mirra will join the Circle. Never my daughter. As you said, she has no magic. But you are allowed. You, a foreigner. After all, Solande has dreamed your presence among us. Why? So you can join the Circle permanently, as Mirra cannot? So you can meddle and interfere in what you don't understand? I wish you'd never come here!"

She spun around and left the barn. Kerstin watched the rich, creamy milk trickle across the floor and into cracks, and also wished she had never come.

CONFRONTATION

Rilka raised her head as Kerstin opened the door of the small shed where medicines were made and stored and plopped down on a chair by the table. Without a word, Kerstin pulled a bowl filled with seneed seeds towards her and began grinding them to make seneed paste, a useful ingredient in poultices. Rilka started to speak, then stopped. The two of them worked in silence for the rest of the afternoon, then walked, still in silence, towards the Circle. The rain had stopped.

Gilles arrived late for supper. The other sisters took one look at her darkly brooding face and left her in peace. Kerstin was surprised when the woman stayed in the hall when the meal was finished, rather than stalking off to her chamber. She started to leave herself, then settled more firmly into her chair. Why should she be reluctant to meet Gilles' eyes? She had only tried to help.

Amary broke into the low-voiced conversations. "We must talk about the situation in Morn," she announced. "Teira has just returned from her visit there and has matters of import to relate."

All eyes swung towards Teira. The young woman leaned forward in her chair, dark eyes intent, smooth face graver than usual.

"It's the sailors from Freya," she said. "They — or rather some of them, for many are helpful and co-operative — lounge about, refusing to work, and force their attentions on the young women, which angers both the women and their families. It's even worse in the few cases where the women welcome the attention," she added wryly. "Tempers are high, and fights break out constantly, despite the best efforts of Mir and the Freyan captain."

She paused, a small frown puckering her brow, then continued slowly. "The fighting and bickering are less troubling, though, than the friendship that has developed between some of the Freyan troublemakers and our own men. The men spend hours together, drinking and talking. I know this worries Mir and others."

"When we were in Morn, there was bad talk about the Circle," Rilka said.

Teira nodded. "There still is."

"I had thought," Amary said, "that we could ignore the situation. After all, the Freyans will not be with us much longer. You are planning to leave soon, are you not?" she asked Kerstin.

"In another month," Kerstin mumbled, looking down at her hands.

Amary nodded, then continued. "However, it now seems to me that we must deal with this matter before it gets completely out of hand."

"What can we do, if Mir and his council and the Freyans' own captain can't control them?" Evita asked, frowning.

"That is what we must decide."

There was a thoughtful silence.

"Perhaps Alannis could use mind-speech to talk to them sternly," Kirilee suggested in her low, husky voice.

Jaine grinned. "Hearing a voice in their minds would certainly frighten them."

"I'd be delighted to do it," Alannis said. "But what if they don't listen, or don't stay frightened? What then?"

"Threaten them with dire consequences if they don't behave," Evita said.

Amary shook her head. "It is senseless to make threats unless we are prepared to act on them. And what threats are we prepared to carry out?"

I could threaten to turn Swain Netter into a fish, Kerstin thought. But she didn't think the Wise Women would appreciate this idea.

Solande confirmed her suspicion. "We cannot use our magic to harm them," she said quietly. Everyone nodded, a few reluctantly.

"Make them leave now," Gilles said. The other sisters stared at her. "Why not?" she challenged. "It's the only way to rid ourselves of these troublemakers who disturb our peace."

Is she referring to the sailors or to me, Kerstin wondered. She shifted uneasily in her chair.

Everyone was silent. No one looked at Kerstin.

Amary broke the silence. "It would not be fair to punish our Freyan guests for the actions of a few unruly men."

"It's not fair, but it may be the best answer to our problem," Alannis said thoughtfully. "I have nothing against you," she assured Kerstin. "It's been a pleasure having you here. I've even enjoyed teaching your father and Ben, though I never thought I'd see men beyond the Sacred Grove. If we cannot control these sailors, however, Gilles' solution may be the best one — even the only one."

Kerstin opened her mouth to protest, then closed it. She'd been longing to leave for the last three weeks. Why should she resent being asked, or even told, to go? She did, though.

Kirilee turned to her with an anxious frown. "How would you and the men feel about leaving early? Have you learned enough?"

Kerstin fumbled for words. She wasn't even sure of her own thoughts, her own desires, much less her father's and Ben's. How could she speak for them all?

"You have taught us a great deal," she said slowly, "and we are very grateful. There is much more we could learn, of course, though we could not absorb all your knowledge if we stayed forever. I — we would like to stay," she said, though she wasn't sure of the truth of this for any of them, least of all herself. "If, however, our departure will help, then we will go." Surely her father and Ben would agree.

"No!" Rilka cried. Everyone stared at her. "I'm sorry," she said more quietly. "But there's still so much to teach them. There are some plants, too, that haven't bloomed yet. They produce medicine I want to give them when they leave. And — "

"And you don't want Morgan to go," Gilles said.

Kerstin's breath caught. How did Gilles know? Did they all know? The silence was brittle.

Rilka looked at Gilles, her face white.

Kerstin's hands were clammy. She felt sick. This was her fault. If she hadn't made Gilles so angry . . .

"It's true, isn't it?" Gilles continued relentlessly. "You've fallen in love with Morgan and he with you, so you don't want him to leave."

"Gilles!" Amary's voice cracked like a whip. "This is no way to speak."

"Why not? Are we in the Circle to be blind, deaf and dumb? Are we to pretend love doesn't exist?"

"Better to be dumb than to speak words that hurt your sister." Solande's usually gentle voice was stern.

Gilles whirled on her, eyes blazing. "Does speaking the truth hurt so much? Does it hurt more than living lives shattered by the Circle?"

"Gilles . . ." Voice trembling, Solande reached out an old, gnarled hand.

"No! Don't touch me, you who wrecked my life!"

Solande's hand dropped. "I told you what I saw in my dreams," she said softly. "I'm sorry if that wrecked your life."

The room was raw with emotion, so quiet that Kerstin heard the thudding of her heart.

Amary stirred. "Is your life truly wrecked, Gilles?" she asked gently. "Are you that unhappy with us?"

Gilles stared at her, eyes dark, and said nothing.

"Would you like to leave?"

"Leave? You mean . . . leave here? Return to Mir and my children?"

"We would hate to lose you, and the Circle would be incomplete without you. There is no one to replace you. But the choice is yours. It always was yours. We could never have forced you to be one of us: you know that. Nor can we force you to stay. Do you wish to go?"

Gilles continued to stare at her. Minutes passed.

"Well?" Amary's voice was quiet, but so full of power and authority that Kerstin shivered.

Slowly, Gilles shook her head. There was a collective sigh of relief.

"No? Good. Since you have freely decided to stay, you must make peace with your sisters. I think an apology is owed to both Solande and Rilka."

Gilles hesitated. Watching her, Kerstin thought how hard it must be for someone so proud to apologise. Then the woman turned to Solande.

"I'm sorry," she said simply. After a moment, she added, "I think I will always curse your dreams a little. But I had no right to blame you, in my words or in my thoughts. I know you meant me no harm."

Solande smiled, a bit tremulously, and nodded.

Gilles looked across the room at Rilka. "As for you, Rilka, who have always gone out of your way to be kind, I am sorry if my words hurt you. I was angry, angry and upset, and I lashed out. Please forgive me."

"No," Rilka said loudly. There was a startled murmur.

Rilka flushed. "I'm sorry, Gilles. I didn't mean . . . Of course I forgive you. What I meant . . . There's nothing to forgive. Why should I blame you for speaking the truth?"

Kerstin's nails dug into the soft flesh of her palms.

"Rilka," Amary began warningly.

"No. No, please. Now that this has been brought out into the open, let me speak. It is a relief, after being silent so long."

"It is true, then? You love this Freyan wizard?" Alannis sounded surprised, even puzzled.

Rilka nodded silently. Tears were falling slowly down her cheeks. She made no move to brush them away.

"But you know — ," Alannis began.

"Oh, yes, I know. No man can be allowed within the Circle. But even knowing that there was no hope, no future, I could not stop loving him." Rilka spoke with quiet dignity.

"Curse the day these Freyans arrived." Teira's voice cracked with distress.

Kerstin stared at the floor and wished she could disappear. Jaine, seated beside her, reached out a reassuring hand. "She doesn't mean you."

Rilka looked at Kerstin. "I'm sorry, Kerstin. I shouldn't speak of this with you here."

Kerstin cleared her throat. "Why not?" She forced herself to look up, tried to make her voice sound matter-of-fact, adult. "It affects me. And it's not as though I didn't know."

Rilka nodded. "I thought you did." She glanced at Teira. "I cannot curse the day the Freyans arrived. It brought me a good friend in Ben Grantwish, an excellent pupil — and I hope a friend — in Kerstin. And it brought me love. I can't regret that, no matter what the pain."

Kirilee reached over and took Rilka's hand in hers. Rilka held it tightly. Kerstin swallowed.

"You, like Gilles, have a choice, Rilka," Amary said quietly. "You may stay, or you may leave and go with Morgan."

Kerstin's head jerked towards Amary. What was she saying? Rilka could go? She and Morgan could marry? Her head swung back. She stared at Rilka.

Rilka shook her head. "I could never leave. What would become of the Circle? What would become of the sick?"

Was that a stab of disappointment she felt? Surely not. She didn't want her father to marry Rilka. Did she? Rilka could never take her mother's place in her home, in her heart.

No. But she could take a place as a friend, a welcome friend, a valued friend.

Kerstin blinked, surprised and wondering.

Evita broke the silence that followed Rilka's words. She was as upright as always, but there was an unusual hesitation in her voice. "I can't imagine weaving the Circle together without nine sisters. Has it ever happened that anyone has left the Circle through other means than death?" Her eyes were fixed on the tapestry on the wall. Kerstin's gaze followed hers. She tried to imagine the weaving with a gaping hole where the warm yellow and soothing blue threads connected with the threads around them.

Kirilee thought. "Once or twice," she said slowly. "During the time of the Mother Peris one left, and the Circle was weakened for many years before a successor could be found. But another time, a new sister was ready almost immediately and no harm was done."

"Would you leave if another Healer could be found?" Jaine asked gently.

Rilka hesitated, then nodded.

Jaine sighed. "Is there anyone ready to become a Healer?" she asked Solande.

The Dreamer shook her head. "I have dreamed, yes. But my dreams have been so strange . . . so confusing. I do not think . . . No."

Raven was a Healer. Kerstin opened her mouth, then closed it. She had made a promise.

Besides, no one would believe her.

"Solande dreamed that Kerstin would come here," Teira said suddenly. "Why? Is it possible she might be the next Healer?"

Kerstin stared at her, stunned. She was not the only one who was shocked.

"Kerstin is an outsider," Alannis snapped.

"Never in the history of Islandia — " Evita began at the same time.

"But Solande did dream Kerstin's presence here," Teira insisted. "That dream has always forecast a new sister."

Stay here? Become a sister? Never return to Freya again, to walk the streets of Frey-by-the-Sea and live in her beloved home on Wizard's Hill? Never see her friends again? Or Rainy? Or Alaric?

Amary looked questioningly at Solande.

The Dreamer sighed. "I do not know. I never understood why I dreamed Kerstin's presence among us. I only know that it was important that she be here."

Kerstin stared at the old, lined face, golden in the lamplight, and clenched her fists. But they can't make me stay, she assured herself.

Amary said Gilles and Rilka have a choice. And I'm not even Islandian.

"No!" Rilka sprang to her feet in protest. "Teira, I know you are thinking of my happiness, but Kerstin has her own life to live, in her own land. She can't stay here. I will stay, as I said."

"Besides which," Gilles pointed out dryly, "there is the small matter of a gift. While I do not doubt that Kerstin is an excellent pupil — she is talented in many forms of magic — I do not think she possesses the true Healer's gift."

Kerstin had opened her mouth to declare her very definite intention of returning home. Now she closed it again. Why? She would never agree to stay here. Would she? Why not say so, firmly, clearly, decisively?

Was she mad? Was it her pride, stung by Gilles' words, taking possession of her as it had done in the past? Was it reaction to Rilka's pain, and the woman's defence of her? Or was it her memory of her father's defeated face as he acknowledged his hopeless love that made her hesitate?

She would never know. Nor would she ever know what she would have said. Just then, the silence that had filled the room was shattered by the sound of splintering glass.

STONES IN THE NIGHT

Kerstin stared at the rock lying in the middle of the woven rug. It was a large rock. Shards of broken glass lay beside it. She looked up, saw the jagged hole in the window. The echoes of splintering, shattering glass rang in the room and in her mind. The echoes died, and she became aware of tramping feet and muttering voices outside. Amary was on her feet and moving even before a rough voice called, "Yo, Wise Women!" The sisters and Kerstin swarmed behind her as she stepped outside.

A crowd of men stood in front of the Circle. The sun had set, but there was enough afterglow in the sky to make out their forms, if not their faces. There must have been twenty at least.

Kerstin heard shocked gasps from the sisters.

"In the Mother's name, why are you here?" Amary demanded sternly. "You know you are not permitted beyond the Sacred Grove. If our help is needed, ask quickly, then go."

There was some shuffling of feet, and Kerstin saw a few men step back. But a voice called, "Help? It's you who'll need help this night, sister. We don't come asking your help. We come demanding our rights."

Amary peered into the dusk. "Who's that? If you wish to speak, step forward."

The speaker hesitated. Then the man standing next to him gave him a small shove and muttered, "Go on, Aron." Quietly as he spoke, Kerstin recognised his voice. She gritted her teeth. Swain Netter.

Aron moved to stand a little in front of the others, facing Amary. He was a big man, tall and husky. Peer as she might, Kerstin could make out only the dim outline of his face — a blunt nose, ears that stuck out. Had she seen him in Morn? She couldn't remember.

Amary seemed to know him. "So, Aron, you are the spokesperson for this group," she said evenly.

"I guess so."

"Then perhaps you will tell us why you are here."

"To demand our rights."

"You said that before. What rights?"

"Our rights to power." He stopped and cleared his throat. "You have it all, you sisters, and we have to come begging to you when we need help with the weather, or our crops or animals, or a sick child. Why should nine women have all the power and we men none at all?" He had started uncertainly, but his voice had strengthened as he continued, encouraged by the shouts of agreement that met his words.

"But you all know the story of the Beginning." Amary sounded more bewildered than angry. "The Mother handed on her gifts to her nine daughters, and they to their daughters. It is not a matter of choosing power, but of being chosen by it."

"Why should we believe that?" called a voice, slightly slurred, from the back of the crowd. "Maybe it's just a story you made up to keep us quiet."

"Because it is true." Kerstin heard Alannis speak, clearly, crisply, both aloud and in her mind. "We do not choose to be sisters. Indeed, some of us would rather not be. We are chosen because we are inheritors of the Mother's gifts."

All those gathered there must have heard the Speaker's voice inside their heads. Muttered oaths followed her words, and a few men clapped hands to their ears. But none could doubt the honesty of that internal voice. Kerstin saw several men glance at each other and begin to edge away.

"But it's one of you who does the choosing," a voice called out.

Solande stepped forward. "It is the dreams that do the choosing," she said, her old voice weak but unwavering. "I am the Dreamer who does the dreaming, but I do not choose. They do."

"Why should we believe you?" another man shouted. Kerstin saw him stoop and pick up something from the ground. She darted forward and seized Solande's arm, dragging her aside just as a stone hurtled past and thudded into the wall behind them.

Solande's breath came in shuddering gasps as tremors shook her frail body. Rilka hurried over and laid a gentle hand on her arm. "Are you hurt?" she asked anxiously.

Solande shook her head. "No. But . . . I don't understand. Who would . . . " She stopped, her voice shaking.

"Who would throw a stone at a gentle old woman? Who indeed?" Amary's voice, taut with anger, rang out over the suddenly hushed crowd. She added, in a quieter tone, "Thank you, Kerstin. You may well have saved our Dreamer's life. Rilka, Kerstin, take Solande inside."

"I want to stay," the old woman said quietly. She stood straight, but the hand resting on Kerstin's arm was unsteady.

Kerstin was trembling too.

Amary turned back to the crowd. "Is that how you seize power? By throwing stones at someone who's never harmed a soul in her life? Is that what you came for?"

Aron cleared his throat. "No. We didn't come to throw stones, and there'll be no more of it. Do you hear me?" he called, raising his voice to the men behind him. Mutters answered him, whether of agreement or protest, Kerstin couldn't tell.

"As for the Dreamer not harming a soul, I don't know about that," Aron continued. "What about the harm she did Mir?"

Beside her, Kerstin heard Solande draw in a shaking breath. There was a small silence, broken by Amary.

"You say Mir was harmed by Solande — or rather by Solande's dreams. But I don't see Mir here, do you?"

No, Kerstin thought, scanning the figures in front of her. Mir wasn't there. But Raven was, she realised with a start, catching sight of a slight form hovering at the back of the group. When had he arrived? Had he been here all along, accompanying the angry mob to demand his rights? Or had he spied the men through his raven's sharp eyes and followed them, slipping in behind them just now?

If so, he was not the only one attracted to the scene. Hurrying along the path, past the grove, were two familiar shapes. Her father. Ben Grantwish. They must have heard the noise from the healing huts.

Gilles' voice drew Kerstin's attention back to the group around her.

"Since when have you been so concerned about Mir, Aron?" she asked tartly. "As I recall, you were never his friend, but rather a rival. Is that why you're here tonight? You are after power, true enough. But not the power of the Wise Women, which is beyond your grasp. Rather, you seek power over these men, who you think will then choose you as leader. As for the rest of you . . . I see few respectable fishers or craftspeople or merchants. Do you, the riffraff and powerless of Morn, really think yourselves worthy of the Mother's gifts? Or have you listened, over too many mugs of ale, to the promptings of envy and the words of outsiders, riffraff worse than you?"

The words lashed them into silence. Kerstin wanted to cheer. Then, as the silence lengthened, she took an involuntary step backwards. Hostility trembled in the air like brooding thunder clouds.

"Are you going to let her get away with that? Are you going to let all of them get away with pulling the wool over your eyes so they can hog all the power? What are you, men or mice, to allow women to rule your lives?"

Swain Netter taunted. An angry rumble answered him.

Kerstin glanced nervously at the open door behind her. But the sisters remained where they were, with Amary standing in front, hands loosely clasped before her. How could she look so unmoved? Kerstin squared her shoulders and tried to appear equally calm.

"What exactly is it you want of us?" Amary asked. "Even if we would, we cannot give you the power that is within us. That is impossible."

"How do we know that?" someone shouted.

"You notice she said 'even if we would'. That's the truth coming out." Kerstin winced, hearing another Freyan accent.

The men moved closer. Kerstin saw someone stoop, pick up another stone. She tensed.

If she used magic, it would be easy to stop them. Kerstin frantically reviewed a couple of spells, and glanced uncertainly at the women around her. Should she? . . .

"I could turn them into frogs," she murmured, making sure only those near her could hear. "Not all at once. But I could use one man as an example." She knew which one she'd choose.

"No, Kerstin, we cannot hurt them," Rilka said, her voice unusually sharp.

"We must not misuse the gifts the Mother gave us," Solande said.

Gilles snorted. "Toads would be more appropriate." But even she shook her head.

Kerstin subsided.

Another man picked up a stone.

"Wait!" Morgan shouted. He and Ben had run the last few yards. Now they pushed their way to the front till they stood facing the mob. Kerstin wanted to run to them, but didn't. She stood rooted, holding tightly to Solande's hand.

"What do you men want?" Morgan demanded angrily. "These women have done you nothing but good, yet here you are threatening them."

"Keep out of this, Freyans. We don't need to listen to you."

"You've listened to other Freyans, unfortunately, to no-good scum like Netter and Potter," Ben said. "Why not listen to sense?"

"To you, you mean?" a man jeered, and laughed derisively.

"Yes, to me, and to your knowledge of these women. Even I, who've been here only a short time, know how much help they give you throughout your lives. Your good sense will tell you that, by endangering the Wise Women, you endanger the source of the help you need." Ben's tone was easy, conversational. He might have been discussing some academic matter with his colleagues at the College of Wizards.

His words and tone made the crowd hesitate. Kerstin relaxed a little.

"He's right," someone said.

"I knew we shouldn't have listened to Netter," another said, sounding disgusted. "Come on. Let's go."

"Wait!" Aron called. He looked at Ben and Morgan. "You're right when you say the Wise Women have helped us, and that we need their help. But Netter's right too, when he says they keep all the power to themselves. I've been thinking about his words, and I've decided things could be a whole lot better." His eyes moved to the sisters. When he spoke again, his voice was filled with quiet dignity. "Gilles, you were wrong in what you said about me and Mir. We may be rivals, but I respect him, even care about him. Things could be a whole lot better," he repeated.

"We have already told you that we cannot give you the power we were born with," Amary said, a bit sharply.

"You could train us."

His words created a ripple, like a stone skipping through water. Amidst the murmurs and exclamations, Kerstin heard a louder gasp. She turned and saw Gilles staring past her.

Following the woman's gaze, she saw Raven, now standing near the front of the crowd. His head was turned towards Aron. Perched on his shoulder, as though it were an extension of the boy, was the raven.

"What are you doing here?" Gilles threw the thought with such force that it made Raven jump and echoed in Kerstin's head. Everyone who possessed mind-speech must have overheard, for Morgan, Ben, and all the Wise Women turned and looked in Raven's direction. He stepped back hastily. Kerstin would have gone to him then if she hadn't been half supporting Solande. Behind her, she felt Gilles' anger like a living creature.

Amary shook her head irritably at the interruption. "How can we train you? Only those with a gift — "

"You've been training the Freyans, haven't you?"

"That's different," Amary said curtly. "They have magic. Admittedly, their magic is not like ours. But it is magic."

"Are you so sure we have none?"

"Of course — "

"Wait, Amary," Rilka said. "I'm sorry," she added quickly, brushing a strand of hair away from her forehead, "but I've been thinking, ever since I met Delos on Moria. Perhaps people can be trained to heal. While only a very few possess the full, true gift, I think others could be taught herb lore and simple magic. And the same must be true of the other gifts."

In the gathering dark, Kerstin couldn't see the men's reactions. But she saw, and felt, the sisters' surprise.

"That's impossible," Alannis said.

"Is it? Couldn't you, who speak so clearly even to those who have no magic, show the way to those who possess a little?"

After a moment, Alannis said "Hmm" thoughtfully.

"It would take a great deal of our time, time that is valuable," Teira objected.

"But once these others are trained, our time will be better used. Our help will only be needed for major magic."

"If this were possible — and I'm not sure it is — it would mean a great change in our lives," Kirilee said.

"Is change so bad?" Jaine asked. She laughed a little. "I work with the weather, which alters constantly, so I am used to change. It adds excitement. We have already made many changes this year, even allowing two Freyan men beyond the Sacred Grove."

"With harmful effects," Evita pointed out. Kerstin winced. She hoped her father hadn't heard Evita's words. Perhaps not. Evita had spoken quietly.

"This is not the time or place to talk about this," Amary said firmly. She turned to Aron and the dark mass of figures behind him. Some had been following the sisters' conversation intently, but others were moving restlessly. "We will discuss the matter further, in peace and privacy, and inform you of our decision. Now please leave. You have made your views clear and can have no more business here."

Aron hesitated. A few men shifted their feet, ready to retreat. Then Swain Netter raised his voice, hoarse with outrage.

"Sure, go home like good little boys while these women decide your fate. All they want to do is keep all the power for themselves. Can't you see that?"

"You think the Wise Women are like the men in Freya who refuse to allow women any power." Kerstin heard her own voice, her own anger, with surprise. She felt everyone's eyes on her and flushed, but continued doggedly. "You can't stand any woman having more power than you do, can you? And you've managed to talk these men into feeling the same way." She was vaguely aware of a stir in the crowd as two new arrivals pushed their way to the front.

"No! It's not just that. Not just what the sailors said." It was a boy's voice, breaking

287

into shrillness. Raven's voice. "We deserve a chance!"

Kerstin felt Gilles stiffen behind her. Before the woman could speak, however, a man's voice thundered out. "Raven! What in the Mother's name are you doing here?"

It was Mir, who had just pushed his way to the front of the crowd. Beside him, Kerstin made out the figure of Captain Merrigale.

Raven said nothing. Mir continued more quietly, but his words lashed. "I would never have thought you'd be part of this shameful company." He stared at his son for another moment, then turned to face the rest of the gathering. His voice was still taut with anger when he spoke.

"I would not have thought any of you would be here. When Captain Merrigale and I were told that men of Morn had gone with some of his sailors to attack the Wise Women, I could not believe it at first. We followed as quickly as possible to find out what madness possessed you."

"As for my men — step forth, Netter, Potter, Hutch and Swallowdale," Captain Merrigale said coldly. "Oh, yes, I know who's here, even though I can't see your faces. You've caused trouble ever since we set sail, and disgraced the good name of all Freyans. Step forth, I said."

The four men he'd named shuffled their way reluctantly to the front. Captain Merrigale surveyed them in silence, then said, "After you've apologised to the Wise Women, we shall leave."

"We're not on board your ship now," Netter said defiantly. "You can't make us do anything."

"You may never be on board my ship. I could leave you here," the captain said softly.

There was a moment's tense silence. Then Netter muttered "Sorry," not looking at the sisters, and the others followed his example.

Amary inclined her head in acknowledgement of this half-hearted apology. "Accepted. Now, I hope everyone will go and leave us in peace." For the first time, her voice betrayed a touch of weariness.

"Yes, we will all go now," Mir said firmly.

"Mir, wait," Aron protested.

"No!" For a moment, the two men stared at one another. Then Mir added, "If there is anything to be said, we can talk about it later. Now we will leave the sisters in peace, with our very deep apologies."

"But — "

"No." The force of Mir's outrage was having its effect. Already many at the back were fading away. Aron looked around and gave in.

"Very well," he muttered. Then he added, with obstinate determination, "But we do have a grievance that needs to be addressed."

"I have said we will consider teaching others," Amary said shortly.

"Does that include men?"

Amary hesitated, then nodded. "If we agree to this, and if any can be found who possess sufficient magic." Doubt was heavy in her voice.

"Now, if everyone is satisfied, we will leave," Mir declared.

"Please use the guest houses," Amary said. "The hour is late to travel." The last of the afterglow had left the sky, and the moon had only begun to peer above the horizon.

Mir shook his head. "I thank you, no. The moon will soon be bright, and it is best we be home." His eyes rested on his son.

Captain Merrigale looked at the Wise Women. "I am deeply sorry for the mischief my men have created. I assure you, they will be punished."

"I would prefer an assurance that they will create no further mischief," Amary said dryly.

"I will do my best," the captain said stiffly. He turned to the sailors. "All right. Let's go."

Kerstin heard one of the sailors mutter, "This is all your fault, Netter. I should never have listened to you."

Netter kicked the ground savagely. "It's the fault of these women, Freyn's curse on them." His words carried, as they were meant to do.

"At least they didn't turn you into a fish," the other sneered.

Kerstin laughed.

Netter whirled and stood facing her. Kerstin couldn't see his face, but she could imagine the hate in his eyes. She flinched.

Bending swiftly, he picked something up from the ground. Then a stone was hurtling through the air, straight at her.

Broken Promise

Morgan lunged forward, but he was too far away to reach his daughter in time. Nor could any holding spell possibly work its magic quickly enough.

But someone was closer. Rilka flung herself in front of the girl. Perhaps she meant to drag her to one side or push her to the ground. There was no time. The rock hit the Healer's temple with a sickening thud. Without a sound, Rilka fell.

Kerstin stared at the woman at her feet. Dimly, she was aware of a babble of voices, of her father kneeling, calling Rilka's name over and over, of Gilles and Teira kneeling as well, of Solande's frail body shaking beside her. But all she really saw, in the light from the open door, was the dark blood streaming down Rilka's face.

"She's deeply hurt," Gilles reported.

Morgan had stopped calling. He was trying to staunch the blood, using the shirt he had torn off in want of anything better.

"Can she be moved safely?" Amary asked.

"I think so," Gilles said.

"Then best bring her inside to the light."

Numbly, Kerstin watched her father gather Rilka in his arms and carry her inside. The sisters followed, leaving the dark mass of men staring after them.

"Are you all right?"

Kerstin started, then looked up into Ben's concerned face. After a moment, she nodded.

"She'll be fine. Come inside."

She shook her head, seeing the same pictures over and over. The stone . . . the blood. So much blood.

"It's not your fault, Kerstin."

She shook her head again. Somewhere in the darkness she heard Swain Netter say loudly, "I didn't mean to hurt her," and Captain Merrigale's angry retort.

No. Netter hadn't meant to hurt Rilka. He had thrown the stone at Kerstin because she had laughed at him, because, six months earlier, she had used her power to turn him into a fish. Misused her power.

"Come inside," Ben repeated. "Perhaps we can help."

Kerstin didn't think she could help anyone. Nevertheless, she let the wizard take her arm and lead her into the building.

Rilka lay on a low couch. Morgan knelt beside her. Several lamps had been placed close by. Blood spread crimson on Rilka's waxen face.

Kerstin shuddered and looked away.

Solande had sunk onto another couch. Kerstin noticed with vague surprise that Gilles sat beside the old woman, holding her hand. The others stood, staring at the motionless Healer.

Morgan's face, his whole body, was stiff with concentration. How would he feel if, despite his best efforts, Rilka died as Star had died before her?

How would she feel? Kerstin wrapped her arms around herself, but couldn't stop the tremors that shook her.

They stood, or sat, silent, still. Then Morgan's head dropped.

"Is she . . . " Kerstin stopped. She couldn't talk. She couldn't say the word.

"No. Not . . . no. But I can do nothing. There is too much internal bleeding. Too much damage." Kerstin could scarcely hear her father.

"Teira? Except for Rilka, you have the strongest power for healing among us. Can you do anything?" Amary asked.

Kerstin glanced sharply at the young Plant Helper's white, strained face. Had she, like Morgan, been trying to heal Rilka? Had all of the sisters?

"I can't," Teira said. Tears started down her face. "I can't."

One by one, the others shook their heads. Slowly. Reluctantly. Like a wave, Kerstin thought wildly. A wave of shaking heads. Rolling into shore. Drowning her. She closed her eyes.

"Perhaps together," Amary said, but her voice sounded tentative, unsure. "Evita . . . "

Evita's back became straighter than ever. "Yes. I will make a weaving."

"It will not be a complete weaving," Kirilee said, her eyes on Rilka. Her husky voice was full of tears. It made Kerstin want to cry.

"No."

"The Freyans," Alannis said suddenly. They all looked at her. She waved a hand impatiently. "They have magic too, and some knowledge of healing. Rilka was proud of their progress. Add their powers to your weaving."

Evita frowned. "I don't think — "

"Why not?" Jaine challenged. "This is no time to talk about them being outsiders, or Ben and Morgan men. We need all the power we can gather."

"Yes," Evita agreed. "But the weaving goes deep. It works because it is a sharing among sisters who know each other, trust each other, live together. To make a weaving with those we scarcely know, who are in so many ways different from us . . . I do not think it is possible."

"You know Kerstin," Ben said. "She's lived in the Circle with you for some months now. The three of us can link our minds and strengths. Then you need only reach out to Kerstin. That would be possible, wouldn't it?"

After a moment, Evita nodded. "It might be."

"We must not waste time," Teira said. Her face was wet. More tears were falling.

"No," Evita agreed. "I will start the weaving. When all the sisters are threaded together, I will add the Freyans if I can." She bowed her head, closed her eyes.

"Morgan, Kerstin," Ben said quietly. "Bind with me."

It should have been easy. She had done it before.

But not when she was shaking. Not when her father's face was desperate with fear, urgent with hope. If Rilka died, would he blame her forever? Blame her for the stone that had been meant to hit her and had struck Rilka instead?

Steady. She must be steady. She must focus. Concentrate. She took a deep breath. Another. She heard Ben utter the words of the binding spell.

Her father's fear was almost too much. She almost broke contact. Almost ran. Didn't. Dug her nails into her palms. And Ben's mind was there, too, calmer than either of theirs. Steadier. Holding them together.

They were joined. She looked at the sisters, saw some of the tension smoothed from their faces. They must be joined, too. Woven together, in their words. Then Evita's mind touched hers. No, not just Evita's. All of theirs, together. She felt herself drawn in, drawn deeper, deeper still, woven and interwoven into the Circle.

No! It was too deep! She was caught, a fly in a spider's web. She struggled to escape.

"Stop it!" a voice snapped. An internal voice. Gilles' voice. A voice like ice water, slapping her into sense.

Rilka. This was for Rilka. She was not caught. She was part of a weaving, she and her father and Ben. A weaving for Rilka. She stopped struggling, let her mind flow with the others. Entered Rilka's head.

And winced at what she found. Almost faltered. But the others were there, and she went with them, exploring the massive bruising, the extensive bleeding. It was too much. Too much. But they must try.

They did. And for a while, they seemed to be winning. The bleeding slowed. But the tissue was torn so badly . . . They could not repair it. They could not do enough.

Rilka was dying. She heard a sob, and realised it was her own. Felt Ben's sorrow, her father's despair, Gilles' remorse, Teira's grief. All their grief. Too much grief. A wordless lament, husky, tear-filled, sang in her mind.

Rilka was dying, and it was her fault.

No!

Kerstin wrenched herself free of the mental bond, oblivious of the shock it caused herself and her companions, oblivious of the pain-filled faces turned her way as she spun around and raced out the door.

Raven. She must find Raven.

At first, she thought everyone was gone. She could see the flicker of torches far down the path that led to the western hills, and the dark outline of moving shadows. They had a good start on her. Far too good.

Then the darkness in front of her shifted, and Mir stepped forward into the light from the open door.

"Is Rilka . . . How is she?"

"She's still alive, but . . . Is Raven here?"

"Raven? Yes, but why — "

Kerstin stepped further away from the door and peered into the shadows. She saw three or four darker shadows. One was smaller and slighter than the rest.

"Raven?"

The figure stirred.

"Raven, you must help Rilka."

There was a low murmur of surprise from the waiting men. Raven said nothing.

"You must."

"How can my son help the Healer?" Mir asked.

Kerstin waited for Raven to speak. There was silence.

Mir spoke gently. "Kerstin, you are frightened for Rilka. We are all frightened. But you must know that Raven cannot help her. Can't you, or the sisters?"

"No. We've tried, and we can't. We're not true Healers. But Raven is." She was breaking her promise. She didn't care. She couldn't care. Not now.

A muffled snort, quickly suppressed, came from the darkness.

Mir laid a gentle hand on her arm. "Kerstin, I'm sorry. I don't know why you think my son is a Healer, but it is impossible. Believe me, if you and the Wise Women cannot help Rilka, no one can." His voice was weighed down by sorrow.

For a moment, she wavered. Raven had never actually admitted he could heal. Perhaps she had dreamed the incident on the beach.

"No!" She shook off the hand and her own doubt, and looked directly at the slight shadow. She wished she could see his face. "Raven, you know you're a Healer. You healed me."

"No — "

"Yes." She put all her own conviction into the word.

"I . . . I don't know," he stuttered, his voice hoarse, strained.

"Yes, you do. You've known for a long time that you have magic, strong magic, that you can heal. That's what drew you to Atua, made you spy on us, pulled you here tonight. You are a Healer."

"That's impossible," stated one of the taller shadows. Kerstin recognised Aron's voice and whirled on him.

"Impossible? But you came here tonight, asking — no, demanding — to share in the sisters' power. Why, if you think it so impossible for a man to have magic?"

"But — this is different."

"Is it? Then why did you come tonight? Just to throw stones?" Kerstin clenched her fists, feeling bile rise in her throat. She wanted to throw something herself. Anything. She forced herself to take a deep breath and turned back to Raven.

"Rilka is dying." The words came out on a ragged breath. She stopped, waited, then continued. "She may die while we stand here arguing. I don't care whether it's impossible for you to be a Healer. You are one. You must — you *must* — help her."

She heard him swallow. "I don't . . . even if it's true . . . " He swallowed again. "Even if it's true, I've never been taught. I don't know how — "

"You healed me, didn't you?"

He hesitated, then said, so quietly that she could scarcely hear him, "Yes."

Beside her, Kerstin heard Mir gasp. She ignored him. "Then try, Raven. It may not work, I know, but nothing else has worked either. At least try."

In the silence that followed her words, Kerstin felt as though the air itself waited, holding its breath. Then, slowly, Raven moved forward.

"Raven . . . " Mir lifted a hand to place on his son's shoulder. Then he dropped it. Silently, he followed Kerstin and Raven as they entered the Circle.

SOLANDE

Raven stopped in the doorway.

Kerstin turned to him impatiently. His shoulders were hunched forward as though he were trying to draw himself in, a turtle seeking refuge in its shell. This was, she reminded herself, forbidden territory. No Islandian male ever crossed this threshold. And the tension in the room was daunting.

She touched his arm gently. "Come in."

He nodded jerkily and followed her.

Their entrance went unnoticed. Everyone was gazing at Rilka. Kerstin's eyes went immediately to her father's face, then away. Ben, a deep frown between his eyebrows, placed a hand on his friend's shoulder.

"You must let go. There is nothing that can be done."

"Yes, there is." Kerstin's voice rang out loudly in the quiet room, startling even her.

Heads swung her way. Eyes widened at sight of her companion.

"Raven," Gilles breathed. She rose and took a step towards him.

"Raven is a Healer. He can heal Rilka."

In the heavy silence that greeted Kerstin's words, Raven seemed to shrink further into himself. Kerstin swallowed. This was not going to be easy. But then, she had known it would not be. She raised her chin and stared defiantly at the sisters.

"My dear girl, I'm afraid you're wrong." Alannis spoke very gently.

"No I'm not. Raven saved my life. He may be able to save Rilka."

Heads shook slowly. She wanted to scream.

"You don't have to believe me." She forced herself to speak quietly. "What harm can it do to let him try?"

"It can hurt Raven," Gilles said, her eyes on her son. "I do not doubt you have a little power," she told him. "Your link with your raven proves that. But not enough. Not nearly enough. You will be hurt, trying to perform magic you are not equal to and have no training for. And when you do not succeed, you will feel yourself a failure. There is no need for that."

"I agree," Mir said from the doorway. He had followed his son that far.

Was she wrong? Was Raven's magic not as strong as she thought? Rilka was hurt so badly. Perhaps Raven would be harmed, and all to no purpose.

"I want to try," Raven said quietly, raising his head. His cheeks were deeply flushed.

"Raven, no! There's no point," Gilles said.

"The point is, he just may save Rilka's life." Morgan had raised his head. His voice was thick. Thick with unshed tears? Kerstin's throat ached. He rose to his feet, a bit clumsily, and looked at the boy. "If there's even a small chance that he can save Rilka, isn't that all the point in the world?"

There was silence. Kerstin was proud of the way Raven stood there, facing their doubting eyes.

"Perhaps — ," Kirilee began.

"No," Amary said. Her voice was quiet but unyielding. "I'm sorry," she told Morgan. "But there is no chance this boy can help Rilka. And Gilles is right. The attempt could damage him." She walked over and stood beside Rilka. Softly, she brushed a strand of hair off her face. "Let her go in peace."

Teira gave a strangled sob and turned away. Jaine laid a comforting arm across her shoulders. Silent tears streamed down Kirilee's face.

"Please. Please, let me try." Raven's voice cracked a little, then steadied.

"No."

"Yes." The voice was familiar, but different somehow. Kerstin turned and saw Solande on her feet.

"He must try." The Dreamer's quivery voice held the strength of authority.

Amary stared at her. "But, Solande, surely you know there is no chance that this boy can help Rilka."

"He must try," the Dreamer repeated.

Gilles swung to confront the old woman. "You have wrecked my life. Do you want to wreck my son's too?"

Solande faced her steadily. "I do not want to hurt anyone. All I do is say what I see. He must try."

"You are speaking as the Dreamer?" Amary asked slowly.

"Yes."

Amary raised a hand and rubbed her forehead wearily. She looked at Raven. "I cannot believe that you can heal Rilka. It goes against everything I have always believed. If Solande says it must be, however, so it must. You may try, if you are willing. But be warned. There may be danger for you."

Gilles made a small noise of protest. Raven glanced at her, then away. He moved towards the couch slowly. Kneeling, he took Rilka's hand.

"Could we make another weaving to help him?" Kerstin ventured.

Evita frowned. "There is no way we can weave our minds with his, unless he's been trained in mind-speech. Has he?" she asked Gilles.

Gilles shook her head.

"Then no, I'm afraid we cannot," Evita said regretfully. Alannis shook her head as well.

"But even without any training, he can go into another's mind, another's body, to heal," Kerstin protested.

"Even if he can do that, he would have to be taught mind-speech before he could take part in a weaving." Kerstin opened her mouth, but Evita shook her head. "It is so with all the sisters and potential sisters when they first come here. Without such training, a weaving would only distract him. Drain his energy when he needs it most."

Kerstin closed her mouth and went to her father. Together, they stood and watched.

Time passed. Sweat ran down Raven's face. His eyes were closed, and he was breathing in short, ragged gasps. Kerstin realised she was forgetting to breathe, and forced herself to concentrate on inhaling and exhaling. Her father glanced down at her and took her hand. She held his tightly.

Out of the corner of her eye, she noticed that Mir had moved into the room and was standing beside Gilles.

Somewhere, a fly was buzzing.

Raven was so pale. If he were harmed . . . If Rilka died . . .

Why couldn't she save Rilka?

She was forgetting to breathe again. No wonder the room was blurring. Or was it because of her tears?

Her legs ached. But what did that matter? She looked at Rilka's pale face, then away.

The room was so quiet. Only the fly and Raven's ragged breathing broke the silence.

A raven croaked, just outside the door. Kerstin jumped. But of course the bird would be there. Oddly, she found its presence comforting.

Then, slowly, the tension eased from Raven's body. His shoulders drooped and he slumped down. Kerstin caught her breath. Was Rilka? . . .

The woman sighed and stirred, then settled back.

Without knowing how she got there, Kerstin was kneeling by her side. Rilka was breathing easily. Her skin . . . Surely it showed signs of returning colour. Yes. It did. Scarcely daring to do so, Kerstin probed with her mind. The internal bleeding had stopped. The tissue was repaired. She looked up and met her father's eyes. He nodded, a slow smile spreading over his face.

"She . . . is she? . . . " Amary asked.

"She will live," Morgan said.

Kerstin looked at Raven. Alarm leaped into her throat.

"Are you all right?"

His eyes were dazed, unseeing. He raised an uncertain hand to his forehead and pressed it, then climbed unsteadily to his feet. He swayed. Fell.

With a cry, Gilles sprang forward, Mir just behind her. Together they caught their son as he crumpled to the floor. Kerstin stared at him, aghast. Was he badly hurt? It was she who had urged him to do this. She was responsible.

"Raven?" Mir was frantically feeling for his son's pulse.

Ben laid a steadying hand on his arm. "Let me."

Mir looked at him uncomprehendingly, then moved slightly so that Ben could kneel beside him. After a minute, the wizard smiled.

"He's exhausted, and I fear he'll suffer from a very bad headache when he awakes. But aside from that, he's fine."

Gilles raised blazing eyes. "Of course he's exhausted. He did a major healing with no training and no help. Even Rilka would have bonded with us to give her added strength for such a work. It's no wonder he collapsed." She looked down at her son. When she spoke again, her voice was soft with wonder. "But he did it. He healed Rilka."

"He is a Healer," Solande said.

"Yes." Gilles stroked Raven's hair, then looked at the Dreamer. "Is that why you dreamed as you did? Dreamed I should marry Mir? Because Raven would inherit my power?"

Solande shook her head. "I told you, I have no idea why I dream as I do. I never knew why my dream hurt you, nor why I dreamed Kerstin's presence in the Circle." She looked from Kerstin to Raven, then back. "But now I think I understand."

Evita spoke thoughtfully. "Raven undoubtedly inherited power from you, Gilles. But it is Mir's family that bears the gift of healing. It is through his father that Raven gained his gift." She shook her head, amazed. "All our ideas are overturned."

Mir cleared his throat. "Is he to be the next Healer, then?" His voice shook.

Solande looked at him compassionately. "I think so."

"You think so? Have you dreamed this?" Amary asked.

"For some time, I have had confusing dreams. I see someone walking towards me, someone I know will be one of us. But when I look closer, I cannot see the face. Perhaps my vision was clouded because I could not believe a boy would be part of the Circle."

"If you cannot see the face, why do you think it is Raven?" Amary demanded.

Solande smiled faintly. "Because when the figure turns to go, I bend and pick up a raven's feather. I did not know, before tonight, what this meant."

As though to echo her words, there was a harsh croak and flap of wings as the raven flew in through the open door and landed on the floor beside Raven. Laughter broke the tension.

Even Amary smiled, the smile lighting her weary face. "We have never had a raven here before — a raven of any kind. But then, we have never had a man inside these walls either." Mir shifted uncomfortably and started to stammer an apology, but she waved him to silence. "No matter. Your presence is only a small part of what has happened lately. And it seems we are about to suffer even more of a — sea change, shall I say? Jaine says change is exciting, but I confess I find it rather overwhelming. I think we should all have some rest. Mir, would you accompany Morgan and Ben to the guest houses? I assure you, both Raven and Rilka will be well cared for," she added, as Mir and Morgan both opened their mouths to protest.

"I'll stay with them," Gilles said quickly.

"Very well. Mir, please lift your son onto one of the couches before you leave."

Mir did so, very gently.

Amary continued, her voice dragging a little. Kerstin thought she looked very tired. "We must make some very important decisions, that is clear. But that can wait for a day or two. For now, I suggest we all go to bed and to sleep."

Kerstin, suddenly exhausted, was happy to follow her suggestion.

DECISIONS

Kerstin wrapped her arms around her upraised knees and glanced sideways at Mirra. The two girls were sitting under a tree in the Sacred Grove. The day was sticky with heat, and Kerstin was glad of the shade.

"I wonder how much longer they'll be," she said.

Mirra shrugged. "Who knows? They've been talking all morning. I wish they'd at least break for lunch. I'm getting hungry."

"Me too," Kerstin sighed. She plucked a blade of grass and nibbled the end. "I don't see why we can't be there. Raven is, after all. So are my father and yours."

"They're directly involved," Mirra pointed out.

"So are we. And we could just sit and listen if they don't want us to speak."

"You'd sit without opening your mouth?"

Kerstin grimaced. "Probably not," she admitted.

"Master Grantwish wasn't allowed either."

That was true. Excluded from the council, Ben had sat with Kerstin and Mirra for a while until he couldn't stand sitting still any longer. Kerstin could see him now, sitting on his haunches in the herb garden, vigorously pulling up weeds. It made her tired just to watch him.

It was three days since the night Rilka was hurt. The Healer had woken the next morning, tired but healthy. Raven had taken longer to recover, remaining unconscious the whole next day. Aron had sailed to Moria with messages for Captain Merrigale and Mirra, and Mirra had arrived in Atua very quickly. She had watched her brother's still face with quiet, fierce concern. Even after he regained consciousness, Raven had been pale and subdued.

Now the Wise Women were meeting to make some decisions. Decisions about Raven's future, about Rilka's future, about the future of the Circle itself. And Kerstin and Mirra were excluded.

Kerstin glanced at the other girl again. She started to speak, then stopped.

"What is it?"

"I was just wondering . . . How do you feel? About Raven having magic, I mean?"

Mirra frowned down at the ground and made circles in the grass. "I've been wondering myself," she admitted. "I'm pretty mixed up. I'm glad there was a reason for Mother's and Father's marriage. I don't have to feel guilty any longer. But I guess I'm a little jealous. Why Raven, not me? I'm the one who should have inherited magic." She paused, then smiled a bit sheepishly. "Not that I want to be a Wise Woman. I'd much rather manage our boat-building shop. And I do want to marry and have children some day."

Marry. Yes. What was Alaric doing right now? What was he thinking? Feeling?

"Will Raven want to be — well, not a Wise Woman exactly. I guess they'll have to change that name if they admit him. Will he want to join the Circle?"

Mirra considered. "I think so. He's too much like Mother not to."

Kerstin thought about this and agreed. Then she said slowly, "You know, from what I saw of them the other night, and from — well, from how I feel — I don't believe Raven's talent is the real justification for your parents' marriage. I think it's just that they had that time together, and two children whom they love." She remembered Rilka's words. "I think their love made even the pain of parting worthwhile."

After a moment, Mirra said, "Maybe." She added, a little shakily, "Thank you."

They had to wait another hour before two figures emerged from the Circle. Kerstin rose, her legs tingling as blood returned to them, then waited impatiently while Morgan and Rilka stopped to talk to Ben. She could have gone to meet them, she supposed. But somehow it seemed important to hear their news here, among the trees of the Sacred Grove.

They seemed to take forever. Then Ben slapped Morgan on the back, and the couple turned and walked towards the grove.

They were smiling.

Her knees went weak with relief.

"They agreed?" she called.

Morgan nodded.

"Is Raven going to join the Circle?" Mirra asked.

"Yes," Rilka said. "In the end, there was no real decision to be made. It may be strange to have a male within the Circle, but it would be unthinkable not to accept the Dream and the Mother's choice. You don't mind, do you?" she asked, her brown eyes anxious.

Mirra shook her head. "No. I'll miss him, of course, and so will Father, but I think it's where he belongs. And it will make Mother happy."

"Yes. As for missing him, one of the decisions made today was that the sisters — or, rather, the members of the Circle, male and female," Rilka corrected herself, "will spend much more time on the other islands, teaching, as well as having pupils here." She sent a mischievous smile Kerstin's way. "The pupils will have to weed and do other tedious tasks, I'm afraid, not only learn magic."

Kerstin returned the smile, a bit sheepishly.

"Your father and brother will be here in a minute," Morgan told Mirra. Just then, the door of the Circle opened and Gilles, as well as Mir and Raven, emerged. Mirra gave a small cry and ran towards them, an arrow shooting straight and true for the gold.

"They'll be all right now," Morgan said softly. "All of them."

Rilka nodded.

"Kerstin, we have to make some decisions of our own," Morgan said.

"We do? What decisions? You and Rilka are going to marry, aren't you?"

Her father smiled. "Yes."

"I hope our marriage will not make you unhappy," Rilka said, her eyes steady on Kerstin's face.

"Unhappy? No. No, I . . . I'm glad." Kerstin smiled at Rilka, a bit shyly. Then, impulsively, she threw her arms about the woman and hugged her. Rilka returned the hug, eyes shining.

"Do I get a hug too?" Morgan asked.

Kerstin laughed and hugged her father. "Congratulations."

"Thank you."

"So what decisions have to be made?"

Morgan sobered. "Decisions about the future."

"I'll have to teach Raven as much as I can," Rilka explained. "It will be at least a year before I can leave him, even though he has a great gift."

"Merrigale wants to set sail as soon as possible," Morgan said. "Understandable, after the last incident. He will come back next year. So we have three choices, Kerstin. We can both leave with him now, and I'll return in a year's time for Rilka. After that, we will divide our time between Freya and Islandia. That's the first choice. The second is that we can both stay here until Rilka feels she can leave Raven on his own."

Kerstin had heard little after the news of Captain Merrigale's immediate departure. If they left now . . . She could go to Uglessia, before the snows fell. She could see Alaric. She heard her father's final words, though, and stared at him, appalled. She couldn't stay here. He couldn't ask it of her.

Morgan continued. "The third option is one I don't much like, but . . . I can stay here and you return home with Ben and continue with your studies by attending the College of Wizards. I'm sure you'd have no trouble being admitted — nor Alaric, when he returns from Uglessia. And Ben said he'd be happy to supervise you and make sure of your well-being."

The College of Wizards. Well, maybe, if Alaric went there too. But not now. She shook her head decidedly. "No."

"No? You'll stay here, then?"

"No. It's all right," she said quickly as she saw her father and Rilka exchange a glance. "I don't expect you to return to Freya with me. I'll sail home by myself. But since I'll be returning earlier than planned, I can go to Uglessia before the snow comes. I'll help teach magic to the Uglessians, as Yrwith asked."

"But — "

"There's no problem. I can accompany Master Bourgly when he visits Uglessia."

Morgan considered this, brow furrowed. "All right," he said finally. "If Master Bourgly is in Freybourg when you arrive, and if he plans to leave for Uglessia anyway. But you must promise to let Ben decide whether it's safe to go, and abide by his decision."

Kerstin nodded eagerly.

"Very well then." He didn't look overjoyed by her choice, but he accepted it. "Let's go tell Ben."

Kerstin blinked as they left the shaded grove for the bright sunlight. Raven and his family were clustered in a small group, talking together. When he saw Kerstin, Raven broke away and came striding towards her. He was still pale, but he was smiling, and there was a light in his eyes that she had never seen there before.

"Thank you. If it hadn't been for you . . . "

"It's I who owe you thanks. And an apology. You saved my life, and I rewarded you by breaking my promise and causing you pain. If it hadn't been for me, you would never have attempted magic you weren't trained for."

He shook his head impatiently. "I wasn't badly hurt. Anyway, I'm fine now. But if it hadn't been for you, I would never have been allowed to join the Circle. I would never have had the courage to admit to anyone, even myself, that that's where I belong."

"You *are* glad to be joining the Circle, then?"

He nodded. "Yes." After a moment he added soberly, "I'm still scared. I know there'll be times when I feel I don't belong here. Maybe most of the time at first. But then, I never felt I belonged in Morn, either — not really. And now I can finally learn all the things I've always longed to know. I can be . . . " He paused, hunting for the right word. "Fulfilled."

Kerstin felt a smile spread over her face.

Raven's family joined him. Gilles looked at the Freyans. "I was right when I thought you'd cause major disruptions," she told them. Then she added with a sudden, swift smile that made her look almost mischievous, "But disruptions can be good. Very good. I'm happy that you came."

"Are *you*?" Rilka asked Mir.

He nodded. "I think so. I don't want to lose Raven, of course, but I won't be losing him entirely. And I think it's the best thing for him. For them," he amended softly, glancing at Gilles.

"You'll be staying here, won't you?" Raven asked Kerstin. "For a while?"

She shook her head. "No. I'm returning with Captain Merrigale."

He was silent for a moment, then said, "Oh." Flatly.

"Are you sure you won't stay?" Mirra asked.

Kerstin started to nod, then paused. The expression on Raven's face hadn't changed, but he looked as though a light had gone out within. He had said he was afraid, that he would feel he didn't belong much of the time. He was right. The sisters had allowed him inside the Circle, but try as they might, they would find it difficult to include him as one of them. It would be easier if another outsider were there, an outsider whom he knew and trusted.

But she wanted to go home. She wanted to see Alaric. Raven would manage. He would gobble up the knowledge he was offered like a hungry man finally given food. She knew how intense his desire was: she shared his longing to learn, to *know*.

Or did she? Here she was, leaving Islandia when there was still so much to learn.

But she wanted to be with Alaric.

Raven had saved her life. And she had broken the promise she'd made him. Now she could redeem herself. She could help him.

Yes. That was true. But she *needed* to be with Alaric. Alaric, who was falling in love with Redelle.

Because of her, Raven was joining the Circle. And he was frightened. Happy. Fulfilled. But frightened.

But —

She was responsible.

Kerstin took a deep breath. "I've changed my mind," she announced. "I'm staying."

She was rewarded by smiles and exclamations of delight from everyone. Ben, who had joined them, clapped her on the back and said, "Good girl. I'd be staying too if I didn't have to go back to teach at the College."

But her true reward was the light that returned to Raven's eyes.

Standing on the wharf in Morn two days later, Kerstin watched the Freyan ship get smaller and smaller. The day was bright with sunlight. Jaine had made sure that they'd have good sailing weather as they left Islandia. Ben, an excellent weather wizard, would take care of the rest of their voyage. And Captain Merrigale, still grim-faced, had guaranteed his sailors' good behaviour, though, in truth, the men had been so subdued since the night of the stones that there seemed little danger of trouble anyway.

Ben was carrying letters from both Morgan and Kerstin to Alaric. Kerstin had found it difficult to write. After pouring out her feelings in her first attempt, she had torn it up and tried again. The second letter was shorter and more formal. After giving Alaric an outline of what had happened and why she was staying another year, she had added her hopes for his health and well-being. Then, after hesitating a long time, she wrote simply, "I miss you."

Morgan slipped an arm around her shoulders. "Not regretting your decision, I hope."

Kerstin stared after the disappearing ship. She could be sailing across the sea to Freya, going where her letter would go. But the ship would return next year, Captain Merrigale had promised. And if she were on this ship, she wouldn't have a chance to learn more from the Wise Women. She wouldn't have a chance to help Raven grow into his new power, his new life.

She shook her head, and glanced behind her at Morn, sparkling in the morning sun, and at Atua, its dark hills rising above the sun-flecked water of the channel.

"No. I'm glad I'm here."

LINDA SMITH is the children's librarian at the Grande Prairie Public Library. She obtained a B.A. from the University of Calgary, a B.L.S. from the University of Alberta, and an M.A. from the Center for the Study of Children's Literature, Simmons College in Boston. Smith has attended several workshops and has had her stories published in Canadian literary magazines and broadcast on CBC radio's *Anthology*.

Wind Shifter, the first book in *The Freyan Trilogy*, was published by Thistledown Press in 1995.

Printed in May 1999 by

in Longueuil, Quebec